MYSTERY
OF THE
ROMAN
RANSOM

OTHER BOOKS BY HENRY WINTERFELD

Detectives in Togas

Castaways in Lilliput
Trouble at Timpetill

MYSTERY
OF THE
ROMAN
RANSOM

Henry Winterfeld

Illustrated by Fritz Biermann
Translated by Edith McCormick

AN ODYSSEY/HARCOURT YOUNG CLASSIC
HARCOURT, INC.
San Diego   New York   London

For information about permission to reproduce
selections from this book, please write
Permissions, Houghton Mifflin Harcourt Publishing
Company, 215 Park Avenue South, NY, NY 10003

www.hmhbooks.com

First Harcourt Young Classics edition 2002
First Odyssey Classics edition 1990
First published in the United States in 1971

Library of Congress Cataloging-in-Publication Data
Winterfeld, Henry.
[Caius geht ein Licht auf. English]
Mystery of the Roman ransom/Henry Winterfeld; illustrated by Fritz Biermann;
translated from the German by Edith McCormick.
p.   cm.
Originally published: San Diego: Harcourt Brace Jovanovich, 1971.
"An Odyssey/Harcourt Young Classic."
Summary: The purchase of a slave for their teacher leads a group of
schoolboys in ancient Rome into a dangerous intrigue.
[1. Rome—Fiction.   2. Mystery and detective stories.]
I. Biermann, Fritz, ill.   II. McCormick, Edith.
III. Title.
PZ7.W766My   2002
[Fic]—dc21   2002024386
ISBN 0-15-216313-1   ISBN 0-15-216268-2 (pb)

Printed in the United States of America

DOC 10 9 8 7 6

4500376494

*For my grandson
Dorian*

Contents

MYSTERY
OF THE
ROMAN
RANSOM

1

Xantippus Can't Use a Lion Either

"Have you lost your minds completely?" Xantippus snapped at his pupils. "By Jupiter and all of the immortal gods, what am I supposed to do with a slave? After contending with you the whole day long, I'm glad at last to be alone and have a little peace when evening comes. Or maybe you want to play a trick on me. A thousand cats on your backs!" he threatened, and cast a suspicious look at the slave cowering, motionless, on a chair in the background.

The boys were hurt. They thought Xantippus would be delighted with a slave. Instead, he was snarling at them. So that was their thanks for having saved their pocket money for months to give their teacher something extra nice for his fiftieth birthday!

Xantippus's real name was Xanthos. A well-known mathematician, he was in great demand as a tutor for the sons of rich Roman patricians. Because he was expensive and exclusive, he had at

present only seven pupils. These were Mucius, Caius, Publius, Julius, Flavius, Rufus, and Antonius. They all lived on the Esquiline Hill, where many rich senators kept luxurious villas. The boys had given Xanthos the nickname Xantippus because he reminded them so much of Xantippe, the wife of the world-renowned Greek philosopher Socrates, who is said to have soured her husband's life with her ceaseless nagging. Xantippus soured his pupils' lives. He was a crabby, hard taskmaster, and he was rarely satisfied. Today once again he was showing his blackest side. The boys had been so proud of their slave idea that they had brought him along to school this morning. They had even gone so far as to buy him a new tunic. The lessons began before sunrise, and now they were sitting at their desks tired and confused and not knowing what to say.

Outside, dawn was glowing faintly. The streets were empty. A few carts pulled by mules and stacked high with lemons and oranges rumbled over the bumpy cobblestone streets in the direction of the farmers' market at the Tiber River. Somewhere in Subura, the district where the poor lived, a rooster crowed. From a distance, behind Viminal Hill where the Praetorian Guard had their barracks, the provocative call of a military reveille blared from a trumpet. Then it was still again. Only the wind could be heard, rustling in the cypresses on the Field of Mars.

"Mucius, look alive," Xantippus said. "Will you please explain to me what I'm to make of these monkeyshines with the slave?"

Mucius was first in the class and responsible for quiet and order. "The thing is this, Master Xanthos," he cautiously began. "We'd settled by a toss—I mean, we'd settled through unanimous conviction—that you could really use a slave. After all, you have so much to do, and, besides, in your free time you work on your important study of acute angles in the obtuse-angled triangle. We thought a slave could do your shopping, tidy up, keep a lookout in the classroom at night so that you aren't burglarized again like last year, and maybe even cook for you."

"Maybe he could write my mathematical studies, too," Xantippus snapped. "No, my friends, many thanks. A slave would give me nothing but trouble. I'd have to go to the city collector to sign the contract of sale, which would cost me a handsome fee. Then I'd have to go to another office to have him tattooed with my personal coat of arms, which again would cost a fee. Finally, there's a high tax to pay every year for owning a slave. Slaves are for the rich; I can spend my paltry bit of money on better things."

Antonius offered, "I was against the idea of giving you a slave from the beginning, Master Xanthos." He beamed with pride.

"Well, it's a refreshing change to hear something so reasonable come from your mouth, Antonius."

Antonius went on with excitement. "Isn't it? I was going to give you a lion."

"What did you say?" Xantippus glowered at him. But that didn't stop Antonius. Once he got going, there was no stopping him. He always had the wackiest ideas. He saw ghosts and monsters everywhere. Not only that, he even claimed this was the reason Rome crawled with thieves and cutthroats. Of course, a lot of escaped slaves were running around free and so were gangs of rebel gladiators, who sometimes killed innocent citizens just for the fun of it. They often broke into houses, too, plundering them and setting them afire. A lawless time had swept over Rome.

"Did I hear you correctly, Antonius? You wanted to give me a lion?"

"That's right, Master Xanthos. My father knows a Numidian prince who wanted to sell a lion because he needed the money. He just wanted two thousand sesterces, and he was going to throw in a cage, too, for nothing. My father bought the lion to donate to the amphitheater so they can put him in one of the clowning matches, but I could have gotten him for less from my father."

"I can't use a lion, either," Xantippus said. "Or is this just a humane way of yours for getting rid of me?"

Antonius protested this. "Oh, no," he said, "he's completely domesticated. The prince is a friend of my father's. I used to visit him all the time and play with Rameses—the lion's name is Rameses. He doesn't bite. He was raised by humans from the time he was small. It's just that sometimes he will thrash his paws at you. So they keep his nails clipped. Other than that, he's as good-natured as a house cat. But nobody has to know that. With a lion in the classroom, you can be assured there won't be any thieves breaking in."

"I wouldn't come in, either," Xantippus said.

"Too bad we didn't go ahead and get the lion," Publius whispered to Rufus.

Antonius was about to streak ahead with another long anecdote about the lion, but Xantippus shut him up. "Enough is enough," he said, "although I would rather have had a lion than a slave." He took another long look at the slave, who sat motionless on the chair. He was about seventeen, and he seemed big and strong for his age. He had brown hair and blue eyes. The boys knew he had been captured in Gaul by Roman soldiers.

"Where did you pick up the young ruffian, Mucius?" Xantippus asked.

"We bought him from a slave trader named Callon."

Xantippus was astonished. "You bought him? I thought you simply brought him from home."

"Oh, no," said Mucius. "Callon has his shop at the Forum Boarium, though it's just a rundown shack. It's on the Tiber River where the shipyards and granaries are. He didn't have many slaves in stock, I'm afraid. He went to get one from a pit, leaving behind a couple of other slaves who were just sitting there waiting on their pallets of straw. Callon led this one up to show to us, pulling him along by a rope. We liked him a lot. Callon said his name was Udo. Udo looked healthy and strong, so we bought him. We wanted you to have nothing but the best, Master Xanthos."

"A good slave is as hard to find as a tooth in a hen," Julius chimed in.

"Please spare me your witty sayings," Xantippus pleaded, turning back to the young slave. "Hey, you there! What part of the world do you come from?"

Udo didn't speak or move. It seemed as though he hadn't even heard.

"He's deaf and dumb," Publius said. "We wouldn't have gotten him so cheaply otherwise."

"By Archimedes, that's a good one. Not only do you bring me a slave, but you also saddle me with one who's deaf and dumb."

"We . . . ah, we went around to several other traders first," Julius said. "A slave in reasonably good condition costs at least twenty gold pieces. That's almost two thousand sesterces. We didn't have that much."

"What did you wind up paying?"

"We'd saved five hundred sesterces," Mucius said. "Udo was a lucky bargain. We got him for four hundred and fifty. For some mysterious reason Callon wanted to get rid of him as quickly as he could."

"Four hundred and fifty sesterces! Were all the Furies at work on you? What were you thinking to give out so much money for me?"

"But today's your fiftieth birthday," the boys shouted as if in one voice.

"What? My fiftieth birthday?" Xantippus appeared amazed. "Where do you get that?"

"Oh, simple," Julius replied. "We went to the Apollo Library and asked Scribonus, the head librarian, for advice. He was very friendly and recommended a Greek book to us on famous mathematicians. The book gave your biography. It was almost two pages long."

"Yes, yes, I know," Xantippus said, and he relaxed a little. "An excellent piece of work Alexis did, incidentally. Go on, Julius."

"It said in the biography that you were born in 723 in Athens. This is the eleventh of September, and the year is 773. So, figuring out that you are fifty was child's play." He added this last triumphantly.

To the boundless astonishment of his students, Xantippus suddenly began giggling into his beard. Only once in a blue moon did he laugh. He said, "With all due respect to your arithmetic, Julius, I'm sorry I can't say the same for your intelligence."

Julius was wounded. "Why not?"

"It's flattering, of course, to know you think I'm only fifty. Unfortunately, that day came and went a long time ago."

"But that's impossible," Flavius cried. "We saw it in black and white in the book."

Julius suddenly exclaimed, "Ah, I've got it. This writer Alexis had it wrong."

"My good fellows, he didn't have it wrong in the least," Xantippus said. "*You* have it wrong. You aren't considering that that is a Greek book. In a Greek book all of the dates are Greek dates. I covered all that with you in history class recently. Again that proves you never pay attention. The Romans begin their years with the founding of Rome, and Greeks theirs with the Olympiad, which was twenty-two years earlier. Thus, according to Roman time, I wasn't born in 723 but in 701." Xantippus called sharply, "Caius, what do you get if you subtract 701 from 773?"

"Plenty," Caius mumbled.

The boys laughed. Sometimes Caius was just too dumb.

"Quiet," Xantippus roared. "If you're going to laugh every time Caius says something stupid, you won't have any time left to learn."

"From 701 to 773 is 72," Flavius called out proudly; he'd even figured it out in his head.

"Not bad, my son," Xantippus said. "Therefore, I'm not fifty today but seventy-two. So you've gone to all that expense for nothing. Return the slave to

Callon at once and demand your money back. And for the future I decline all gifts—slaves, lions, or anything else. By the way, I'm giving you the rest of the day off," he added with a nervous cough. He immersed himself in a roll of papyrus; for him the matter was settled.

"Thank you, Master Xanthos," the boys shouted in chorus. They leaped from their seats in delight and packed up their schoolbooks.

"We must admit we made a mistake in getting you a slave," Mucius offered politely.

"A real mistake," the others agreed.

Little did they know that it was not merely a mistake but a disastrous error that would nearly cost them their lives.

2

Why Did the Slave Dealer Run Away?

The boys set out at once to take Udo back to Callon's. The slave followed close behind them, to all appearances resigned to his fate. He kept his head down, as though he wanted to avoid being recognized.

It still was early. The edge of the sun was just coming up behind the branches of the pine trees lining the Esquiline Hill. On Broad Street, where Xanthos had his school, only a few passersby were to be seen. Here and there street cleaners, with broom and wheelbarrow, were sweeping pavements. Four slaves trotted past the boys bearing an elegant sedan chair with curtains closed over the windows. A couple of carts that had been delayed on their rounds pressed desperately toward the Tiber bridge to get out of the city in time. By order of the Emperor, no wheeled traffic was permitted in Rome during the day; even people on horseback had to

have special passes to ride through the narrow, crowded streets of the inner city.

By taking a shortcut, the boys avoided crossing the Forum Romanum and marched instead behind the Capitoline Hill, past the Flaminus Circus and the Marcellus Theater. A few minutes later they arrived at the Forum Boarium along the harbor.

In front of Callon's cottage, they pulled up short. The door was barricaded, and the windows were boarded up.

Mucius pounded violently on the door several times, but there was no answer.

"Why hasn't that lazy lout opened up yet?" he yelled.

"He made so much money off us that he's probably sitting around in a sailor's pub," Publius said.

"I'm not leaving until I have our money back," declared Julius.

He was thrifty; that's why his friends had made him their treasurer.

"Something's wrong here," Flavius said. "Otherwise, why would the windows be boarded up?"

Rufus said, "Callon will come all right. Surely he can't let his slaves starve to death."

"That's what you think," said Antonius. "I wouldn't put anything past that rascal. He'd let his slaves starve to death with the greatest pleasure."

Always practical, Publius thought otherwise. "If he lets them starve to death, he won't be able to sell them."

"That's right," Antonius said, looking a bit chastened.

"What do we do now?" asked Flavius.

"We keep on waiting," Mucius said. He sat down on a low wall at the riverbank, and the others followed his example.

Meanwhile, Rome had awakened and work was starting throughout the city. Along the shore carpenters' hammer blows resounded from the shipyards. A galley from the fleet of Roman warships glided past, heading downriver. The long paddles slapped the water to the rhythm of muffled strokes from the slave driver's gong. Near the dock, behind

Callon's cottage, an Egyptian bark rocked gently up and down. Dozens of half-naked slaves hauled sacks of grain on their bowed backs, trudging to the warehouses. Even the covered markets nearby were already open; shouting and the roar of laughter carried over from them to the boys. A strong smell of fish, cheese, exotic spices, and frying sausages seasoned the air. A couple of stray dogs were nosing around in garbage for scraps of meat and vegetables, and they snarled ravenously at each other with bared fangs. The boys looked at them fearfully. There were whole packs of wild dogs in Rome. Sometimes even wolves stole in, too, and made the streets unsafe.

"Why don't we come back tonight?" Flavius asked. The wild-looking slaves, breathing heavily as they tramped by, made him uneasy.

Nobody answered him.

"This Callon business is getting just plain stupid," Caius said. He grabbed a rock and flung it against the door.

Suddenly the door opened a crack, and an old white-haired slave peered out. The boys stormed over to him.

"Hey, open up," Mucius said. "We have to talk to Callon right away."

"What do you want?"

"We were here yesterday," Mucius replied. "We're bringing back the slave we bought."

"Oh, so it's you." The old man pushed the door open and hobbled out on crutches. "Callon isn't here. No one is here."

"Why isn't Callon here?" Mucius asked. "When is he coming back?"

"He isn't coming back. He's fled."

"Fled?" the boys cried.

"Yesterday afternoon he sold all of his slaves in a hurry to another dealer. Then he packed up a few of his things and marched off. Where, he didn't say. I'm the only one left behind. No one would have me." He grinned with his toothless mouth.

"Callon made off with our money," Julius cried.

"By Pluto and all the spirits of the underworld, why did Callon flee?" Mucius asked.

"There was a man here," the old man explained, looking anxiously around as if the three goddesses of revenge—Megaera, Alecto, and Tisiphone—were waiting for the chance to pounce down on him. "The man wanted Callon to give him Udo, the slave. Him there!" He pointed one of his crutches at Udo, who stood mutely behind the boys.

"So we snatched Udo away from him in the nick of time," Antonius crowed.

"Don't celebrate too soon, young fellow," the old slave said. "The man swore he will not rest until he has Udo dead or alive."

"He must be crazy," Flavius said, but he was disturbed.

"That man doesn't scare us," Caius said.

"Don't say that, my son. You don't know him. By Hades, he's a frightening sight. He has only one eye."

"Is he a cyclops?" Antonius cried.

"I think he's a former gladiator," the old man said. "He wears a wooden sword—the sign that he was released from the arena."

Mucius asked, "What does this fellow want from Udo anyway?"

"I don't know. But he asked about you, too, what your names were and where you live."

Involuntarily, the boys turned and looked around uneasily.

The old slave went on. "Callon told him he didn't know who you were or where you lived. He never cared about who his clients were or where they came from. At that the man pulled out a knife and held it against Callon's throat. 'I'm coming back tomorrow,' he said, 'and if Udo isn't here then, I'll kill you and all your slaves, too.' "

"Good Hercules!" Flavius muttered, turning pale.

"You'd better go away," the old man warned the boys. "The man could be here any minute." He hobbled back into the cottage. Before he disappeared into the darkness, he turned again and cried thickly, "Take the young slave there and drown him in the Tiber so you'll be rid of him forever." He slammed the door and blocked it up again.

3

The Fearsome Ex-Gladiator

"I think we'd better get out of here before this one-eyed ex-gladiator shows up," Mucius said.

Perplexed, he started to pull on his nose. Mucius was brave, but he wasn't foolhardy.

"I think so, too," Flavius said.

Nobody protested, and Mucius signaled for Udo to follow. They ran across the Forum Boarium over to the Velabrum—the big, low-lying esplanade between the Capitoline and Palatine hills—and swung into Tuscan Street—the liveliest main street in Rome. It led from the Velabrum to the Forum Romanum, the center of the Roman Empire.

Once on Tuscan Street, the boys felt more sure of themselves. Now they proceeded at a snail's pace. Dense crowds of people pushed along the sidewalk past shops and stalls in an endless chain, among them many foreigners. The city seemed overrun with Greeks, Arabs, Persians, Egyptians, and the most varied mob of wild-looking characters—the boys wondered what enigmatic corners of the world they came from. The roadway was filled with hundreds of sedan chairs—large and small, elegant and shabby, many borne by two, others by six or eight slaves. They were all wedged together like two armies in battle.

The fact was, all traffic had come to a halt. In the Forum the Emperor's guard had just marched past, twelve cohorts from the Praetorian Guard. They were going up the Palatine as relief watch. The Praetorian Guard looked glorious. They wore yellow uniforms with red belts and big earrings and were armed with bamboo spears. The officers had iron helmets decorated with colored feathers, and their breast armor sparkled like polished silver.

The people in Tuscan Street didn't bother much with the Praetorian Guard. It had grown unbearably hot; the sun already was high in a cloudless sky and shone down relentlessly on the pavements. Almost all the women protected themselves with umbrellas. None of the Roman citizens wore togas. They had put on the lightest tunics they could find in their wardrobes. People flailed their arms wildly about to chase away swarms of bluebottle flies descending on them from all sides. The whole area smelled sickeningly from the stockyards at the Forum Boarium, the filthy waters of the Tiber, and the drainage canals of the Great Sewer, which ran alongside Tuscan Street. Rome was not a pleasant place to visit in the summertime.

The boys encircled Udo and bored a path through the crowd like a patrol of legionnaires. Once they reached the Forum, they sighed with relief. They finally had elbowroom again and more air. They sat themselves down on an upholstered bench in front of the Temple of Saturn and wiped the sweat from their foreheads.

Udo sat down on the stone pavement and leaned against the milestone on the speaker's platform. He was panting like a wild beast, too.

"Here we are with Udo like Priam amid the ruins of Troy," Caius said.

The boys were tired, hungry, and irritated. It was not much cooler in the Forum. Even the pigeons roosted lazily on the roofs of the basilica.

"Your comparison stinks," Publius taunted Caius. "Priam didn't have time to spend among the ruins. He was slain by Neoptolemus immediately." Thanks to Xantippus, Publius knew his Homer almost by heart.

"You stink," Caius replied wrathfully.

"Dumbbell," Publius said.

Caius was about to jump him, but Mucius intervened. "No fighting," he said, "or one of you will have to go home. There's no room for two cocks on the same dunghill."

Caius backed off reluctantly. After all, Mucius was the leader of their band; they had pledged themselves to him with a solemn oath and had to obey him.

"Don't get excited," Julius said. "Nothing's lost. We'll simply sell Udo to somebody else."

"What can we hope to get for a deaf and dumb slave?" Flavius said. "Callon took us in."

"It could take us a long time to find a buyer," Mucius said. "It would be smarter to get rid of Udo as quickly as possible."

"Why don't we take him to the island on the Tiber, to the Temple of Aesculapius, where everybody puts out his old or sick slaves?" Caius suggested.

"That would be wrong," Rufus said. "A slave's human, too. We treated Rompus, my tutor, like a friend. My father gave him his freedom later."

"Bah!" said Caius. "A slave isn't a real human being. Last week one of our slaves kissed my sister Claudia on the hand in gratitude because she forgave him for accidentally breaking her favorite cup. My father saw what happened and had a fight with her for letting a slave kiss her hand."

"What happened to the slave?" Flavius asked.

"My father sold him the same day to the amphitheater as a gladiator."

"There's the answer!" Antonius shouted. "Why don't we sell Udo as a gladiator? They can always use new gladiators. They're slaughtered by the dozens in the arena at every performance."

Antonius's proposal inspired the others.

"That solves all our problems," Julius said. "Maybe we'll get even more than four hundred and fifty sesterces for him."

They banded together at once and, cutting across the Forum, headed toward the Via Sacra, where the amphitheater lay. In front of the Triumphal Arch of Augustus they saw a street vendor who was selling figs soaked in honey. The figs were piled in a crate; the honey filled a bronze jug.

Publius stopped, transfixed. "Hey, Julius," he cried, "I'm starving. How about treating each of us to three figs? We still have fifty sesterces left of our spending money. Three figs cost only a copper, according to the sign there."

"Pretty expensive," Julius muttered. But he pulled out his money pouch and counted seven coins. Hesitantly, he added another for Udo. "Here, buy figs for Udo, too," he called to Publius, and handed him the money.

But Publius never got to the vendor. Suddenly, a burly-looking man broke through the circle of people standing around the fig vendor, threw himself at Udo, flung a noose around his neck in a second, and pulled it tight. "By Hades, I've finally caught you, you wretch," he yelled like a raging buffalo.

The boys were petrified. The man had only one eye, and he wore a wooden sword at his belt.

He was the fearsome ex-gladiator.

4

A Surprising Use for Honey

The man began dragging the young slave behind him like a wild horse he had lassoed in an arena. Udo couldn't defend himself, or he would have been strangled.

Mucius shook himself out of his stupor and took a heroic position in the man's path. "Let that slave go at once!" he cried. "He belongs to us."

The man spat his contempt and shoved Mucius aside with his arm.

"Ow!" Mucius shouted, and kicked the man in the shins.

The ex-gladiator didn't seem to feel it. "Get lost!" he barked, exactly like the three-headed dog Cerberus. "Or I'll break every bone in your body."

Now the other boys sprang to Mucius's rescue. Julius, who saw his four hundred and fifty sesterces disappearing forever, grabbed Udo's sleeve and clung to it. But the sleeve tore off, and Julius took a hard seat on the pavement. Caius and Rufus rushed the man and beat him with their fists; Antonius and Publius tried to tear the rope from his hand. At the same time Flavius was dancing around the battlers, pleading for help from all the good gods, from Jupiter all the way down the scale to Ceres.

A circle of spectators had formed. They watched the exhibition with disapproval. Nobody moved to help the boys. Some women started railing at them. "Just another example of the abysmal corruption of our youth today," one woman yelled. "Now they're attacking helpless citizens in the middle of the Forum in broad daylight."

"Someone should call the police," another woman cried, embracing her two little children protectively.

"Wouldn't you know, the police are never around when you need them," a man commented, stuffing a fig in his mouth.

Meanwhile, the fight over Udo was getting more and more violent. Antonius bit the ex-gladiator in the hand to make him release the rope. The man grew really angry. With one movement of his arm he threw Caius, Rufus, Antonius, and Publius to the ground. They tumbled around the vendor's feet as though an elephant had swept them there with its trunk.

Caius, out of his mind with anger, leaped up, grabbed the pail full of honey, and dumped it over the ex-gladiator's head. Shocked, the man dropped the rope holding Udo, and the boys tore off with the slave, the noose still around his neck.

As they ran across the Forum, the only audible sound was the ex-gladiator's low gurgling. They turned into the Subura district and a little farther on rushed up the stone steps to the Esquiline.

"Into our cave," Mucius cried. "We'll be safe there."

He hadn't needed to say it; the boys always ran to their cave for cover when things got hot.

The cave lay hidden on an isolated slope of the Esquiline and was difficult for the uninitiated to find. Safely inside, the boys dropped exhausted onto the wood crates they used as chairs.

"That honey was a stroke of genius, Caius," Publius said, panting.

Caius grinned; praise from Publius was rarer than a good mark from Xantippus.

"You saved our lives," Antonius said between fits of coughing. "If it weren't for you, that gladiator would have killed us all."

"But who can that monster be?" Julius muttered while he struggled for breath.

"And what, by Jupiter, can he want of Udo?" Mucius asked.

Unfortunately, Udo couldn't help them out; the poor fellow was mute.

"What are we going to do with Udo?" Rufus asked. "It's out of the question now to risk going down the street with him."

"There's only one thing to do," Julius said. "To-night, when it gets dark, we'll take him to the police and hand him over."

"Please, young masters, do not do that," Udo suddenly said, simply and distinctly and in the best Latin. "If you give me up to the police, I am doomed."

The boys stared at him with mouths agape. Udo could speak! Flabbergasted, they were the ones who were speechless now.

5

No Respectable Citizen Visits the Cemetery at Night

The boys continued staring at Udo. Why had he pretended to be deaf and dumb?

Muffled street noises carried up to them from the Subura district. The crickets in the grass chirped unceasingly outside their cave.

"Why did you pretend you couldn't speak or hear?" Mucius asked finally.

"Young masters, you must forgive me," Udo said. "If you'd questioned me, I would have had to lie. I was sure you would have seen through that, and I was afraid you would turn me over to the police."

"Confess," Julius commanded. "What crime have you committed that you are afraid of the police?"

"I swear by all the holy gods I have done nothing wrong," Udo said. "But the police would have discovered at once who I am and where I came from." He bared the upper part of his right arm and showed them a tattoo—an eagle with two crossed swords beneath it. "I am the personal slave of your famous hero, Marcius Patricius Pollino."

Rufus shouted, "The commander-in-chief of the Roman occupation army on the Rhine! His headquarters are in a fortress across from Cologne. I learned that from my father. Pollino served under him when my father was still waging war in Germania."

"My master now is one of the most powerful and most feared sovereigns in Germania," Udo said. "If the police discover his seal, they'll send me straight back in chains."

Mucius said, "You mean that you escaped from your master and fled to Rome?"

"No, young man. My master ordered me here to deliver a letter."

"How he lies!" Caius said with disdain. "All slaves lie. If he didn't desert, then why should he be afraid of being sent back?"

"My master would behead me for not delivering his letter."

"Is that so. Then why haven't you delivered it?" Julius asked.

"Because, after passing it over, I would have been killed right here in Rome." Udo disarmed the boys with a smile that exposed radiant white teeth.

"By Romulus and Remus," Publius cried, "not even a Diogenes could have come out of that more slyly."

"How did you learn that somebody wanted to kill you?" Mucius asked.

"I discovered it at the last minute. My master instructed me to go to the second milestone in the Via Salaris around midnight—my master knows I'm acquainted with Rome. For ten years my father was in charge of guarding the wild animals in the amphitheater. I visited him there secretly a few times because I know a hidden passageway into the catacombs under the arena. I went to school in Rome."

"That's why you speak Latin so well," Julius said.

"I was taken prisoner in Gaul two years ago in a battle against Roman legionnaires. Pollino made me his slave."

"Spare us your life history," Caius said.

"That's right," Antonius said. "We want to know why you're supposed to be murdered. That's exciting."

"Why not let him talk?" Julius scolded.

Udo waited a moment, then he went on. "My master said that across from the second milestone in the Via Salaris there was a big open gate I couldn't miss even in the dark. I was supposed to walk through the gate to the first stone building. There I was to wait for two men. They would give me the password, and then I would hand over the letter. The password was 'Croesus.' "

"Croesus!" Antonius said with excitement. "He was the king of Lydia. He was supposed to have been the richest man in the world."

"By Hercules, stop interrupting him all the time," Mucius snapped. "Go on, Udo."

"I followed those instructions faithfully. At midnight I went to the second milestone in the Via Salaris, then through the gate, and looked around for the stone building. As I was looking for it, I got lost in the darkness and fell into a hole onto something soft in a wooden box. I jumped up and discovered it was a dead man in a coffin."

"A dead man in a coffin?" Flavius said, growing pale.

"Why wasn't the coffin closed?" Rufus asked.

"There are criminals who rob corpses," Julius said. "My father gave somebody the death sentence a while ago for just that."

Udo continued. "I climbed out of the hole and sat down on a tombstone. I realized that I was in a cemetery and was afraid to go on. Why, I asked myself, must I deliver a letter in a cemetery at the ghastly hour of midnight? What kind of men was I waiting for? No respectable citizen visits the cemetery at night."

"It's alive with ghosts," Antonius said.

"I decided to hide somewhere around the meeting place and get a look at the two men first," Udo said.

"That was smart of you," Mucius said. "What happened then, Udo?" he asked.

"Warily I crept farther on and almost hit my nose on the stone building. It was a mausoleum. Beside it was a bunch of laurel bushes. I had scarcely crawled behind them when I heard the two men coming."

"Did you see their faces?" Julius asked.

"No, it was too dark. Besides, they were wearing capes with hoods pulled over their heads. I saw only that one man was of average height and fat and the other was as big as Hercules. The fat one must have been disguising his voice, for he spoke unnaturally through his nose.

"I was glad I'd found a hiding place. They both looked conspiratorial. They sat on the steps of the mausoleum and spoke to each other. 'Why isn't this scum of a messenger here yet?' the big man wanted to know. He had a gravelly voice and spoke like a halfwit. 'It's a long trip from Germania to Rome,' the fat one said. 'The mail coach itself is often late.

If he doesn't get here tonight, we'll have to wait
again for him tomorrow at midnight. The letter he's
bringing is very important for me and my friend.
For you, too. It will tell us what you'll have to do
tomorrow.'

" 'Say, potbelly, who are you, anyway?' the big
man roared. 'And who are your other chums?'

" 'None of your business,' the fat man said. 'When
you've finished your job, you'll get your thousand
gold pieces. Then disappear or you'll land in Hades,
too.'

"The big man seemed to be afraid. 'All right,
all right,' he said. 'It's none of my business. I just
want to earn my thousand gold pieces. Who's bringing the letter? Can't I know that either?'

" 'He's a slave named Udo.'

" 'So, Udo, a lousy slave. Slaves are more dangerous than poison snakes. What do we do with him after he's delivered the letter?'

" 'The gods must have struck you blind,' the fat one replied. 'Why do you think we're meeting in the dark in a cemetery? You'll bury him here on the spot.' "

Udo smiled again. "I didn't take much of a liking to their honorable plan," he said. "I retreated noiselessly without delivering the letter and ran through the gate to the street."

"Those two men must be up to something sinister," Flavius said.

"I know what they're up to," Udo said. "The big one is supposed to murder a high dignitary in Rome."

"Great Jupiter," Mucius burst out. "Did you hear who is supposed to be murdered?"

"They don't know yet. That's why they were waiting for me. It would tell them in the letter, according to the fat man. All he said was that it was a famous senator who was supposed to be done away with."

"What?" the boys cried in horror. Each of their fathers was a famous senator.

6

A Fateful Letter

"My father is one of the most famous senators in Rome," Caius said.

"Mine, too," asserted Antonius.

"Quit preening yourselves," Publius said.

"You're the one who's always preening yourself," Antonius replied.

"I'll give you something," Publius said threateningly, and he struck his fist against the crate he was sitting on.

"Ha, ha," retorted Antonius. And he quoted, " 'He who is afraid to beat the ass beats the saddle.' "

"All right. That's true. And you are the ass," Publius countered.

"You're both asses, and I'm going to beat both of your hides in a second," Mucius grumbled. "Don't forget, our fathers' lives are at stake."

Publius and Antonius fell silent. The boys stared

anxiously into space for a while. They loved their fathers dearly. A chunk of lime from the ceiling dropped at their feet, but they didn't pay any attention.

"If only we knew which senator," Caius said.

"We should offer a sacrifice to Jupiter in the Temple of the Moon," Flavius said.

Rufus cried out suddenly, "You've all got blinders on!"

"Why?" the others asked, surprised.

"The letter . . ." Rufus said. "The letter must tell which senator is to be murdered."

Mucius hissed, "Udo, quickly, give us the letter."

"I'm sorry, young master. I no longer have it."

Caius stamped angrily on the chunk of lime. "What do you mean? You told us yourself you never delivered it."

"And I didn't," Udo said. "It's in my cloak."

"Then go and get your cloak at once," Mucius commanded.

Udo sighed. "I'd like to do that, but the cloak is in some cellar where I slept last night, and I don't have the faintest idea which cellar it is."

"By all the Furies, why not?" Mucius moaned.

"Well, it still was pitch dark when I escaped from the cemetery," Udo said. "I ran through narrow, twisting alleys, up hills and down, and finally got hopelessly lost. I was tired, so I stole down some stone steps into a cellar and lay down to sleep behind a couple of barrels. The floor was like a rock, so I took off my cloak, rolled it up, and put it under my head. In the early morning I got a rude awakening. A woman hit me on the head with a broom. 'Help! Murder! Thief!' she shrieked. I started running again and in the scramble left the cloak. I tore blindly around lots of corners. The last one turned out to be my undoing. I bounded into a group of drunken gladiators. They surrounded me and demanded to know who I was and what my name was. I just told them my name was Udo, then kept my mouth closed. They searched me for money. They didn't find any—my money was in my cloak, too. They were so angry that they wanted to beat me. Luckily, one of them had a better idea. 'If we beat the lout, afterward he won't be worth a copper,' he said. 'Let's sell him as a slave, so at least we'll get something out of him.' That's what they did, all right, dragging me off to Callon. They got a hundred sesterces for me, which I consider quite cheap." Udo smiled. "But the gladiators went away highly pleased."

"What a gouger, this Callon," Julius said. "And he fleeced us for four hundred and fifty."

"That's not much for me, either," Udo said, still smiling.

"Perhaps the ex-gladiator who attacked you in the Forum just now was one of the conspirators?" Mucius said.

"That may be. He was wearing a wooden sword, and so was the Hercules at the cemetery. What I don't understand is how he knew I was at Callon's."

"Very simple," Julius said. "As a former gladiator he has a lot of friends among them. One started boasting about their having sold Callon a young Gaul named Udo."

"None of your talk does us any good," Mucius said. "The conspirators themselves still don't know who they're supposed to kill. They're waiting for the letter."

"Udo," Publius said. "Didn't you read the letter?"

"I wouldn't have dared, young master. The letter was sealed."

"That wouldn't have bothered me," Antonius said.

"The fact that Udo didn't deliver the letter is a gift from the gods," Rufus said.

"Unfortunately, the gift from the gods is short lived," Udo said. "My master, the famed General

Pollino, is coming to Rome himself in three days. Then the conspirators will learn from him whom they're supposed to kill."

"Then what was the point of sending you with the letter ahead of time?" Julius asked.

"Because he hoped the famous senator would already have been out of the way. Pollino seems to be in a hurry. His strategy generally is to strike like lightning."

"Oh, dear gods," Flavius wailed. "The man isn't a general—he's a murderer."

"Wait," Julius said. "I think we're all getting stirred up unnecessarily. There are nine hundred senators in the Senate. It's not likely one of our fathers is named in the letter."

The boys breathed more easily.

"A lot of crazier things happen in life," Publius observed, smiling.

"Shut up," Caius said.

Flavius became anxious again. "We should run to our fathers at once and warn them," he said.

"None of them are at home," Julius reminded him. "They're all in the Senate. A vote is being taken on an important proposal concerning an increase in taxes. The session could last all night. And, as all of us know, nobody is allowed in the Senate."

"Should we go to Xantippus and ask his advice?" Flavius suggested.

"Pooh, Xantippus," Caius said. "Again today all he did was rage and fume. I'd have loved to hit him over the head."

"Hitting a teacher is not allowed," Julius said wisely.

"I know slaves who are teachers in schools," Flavius said. "Aren't we allowed to hit them, either?"

"No, that's also forbidden," Julius said.

"That's the end," Caius said. "Next thing you know we won't even be allowed to kill a fly."

"Who's going to kill whom?" a surly voice said. Xantippus stood at the entrance to the cave glowering in at his students.

"Master Xanthos!" Mucius uttered in surprise.

7

They All Are in Danger

"I suspected you had crept into your cave again," Xantippus said.

What did Xantippus want with them, Mucius wondered. He had come to the cave only once before, and that had been once when Rufus had been in trouble. Did their teacher want to help them again? But how could he have known they needed his help?

Xantippus peered around the cave with disapproval; it had offended him the last time, too. "Give me that chair there," he said, pointing to an old easy chair.

Rufus and Flavius dragged over the heavy chair. Disgustedly, Xantippus beat off the dust with his walking stick, then carefully let himself down. He probably still was remembering the dangerously wobbling crate the boys had offered him to sit on during his first visit here.

"Out with the truth," he said, banging his cane on the floor. "What have you done wrong *this* time?"

"Why do you ask?" Mucius ventured. With Xantippus you never knew exactly whether you had sinned or not. "I swear by Castor and Pollux we haven't done anything wrong."

"Aha," Xantippus said. "So you also believe that old maxim: 'The greater the lie, the more readily believed.' The police came to see me about you."

"The police?" Caius and Rufus cried.

"You're supposed to have dumped a jug of honey over somebody's head at the Forum," Xantippus said angrily. "Don't you know honey is expensive?"

The boys laughed.

"Quiet!" Xantippus thundered. Still looking at them fiercely, he said, "The man nearly smothered to death."

"It was particularly sticky honey," Publius said.

"The man wasn't a man, he was a conspirator," Antonius cried.

"He wanted to steal Udo from us," Julius said. "We were only defending ourselves."

Xantippus cast a hasty glance at Udo, who was sitting on the ground listening intently. "Why didn't you take the slave back to Callon the first thing this morning as I told you to?"

"We wanted to, but we couldn't," Mucius said. He told why they couldn't return Udo.

"Then you should have come to me immediately and asked for my advice," Xantippus said.

"But you didn't want him," Caius said defiantly. "If you'd kept him, the police wouldn't be after us now."

Surprisingly, Xantippus allowed this remark to pass without reproach. "I didn't reveal who you are to the policemen," was all he said. "They'd gone to other schools earlier and asked about six or seven boys who had attacked a man in the Forum. Short and to the point, I told them it couldn't have been you because you'd been sitting in school in my sight all morning."

The boys snickered again.

"I hope *that* lie is big enough," Publius whispered to Flavius.

"I'm no police informer," Xantippus continued, "but your behavior in public is, again, the best illustration of your appalling lack of discipline. I'm going to see your parents tonight and have a serious word with them."

The boys were scarcely overjoyed by that prospect.

"Master Xanthos," Mucius pleaded, "please don't

go to our parents. You don't yet know everything. Only by the grace of the gods did we rescue Udo from that man's clutches. It's possible that we've prevented a heinous crime."

Xantippus was astonished. "By Pythia, you speak in riddles, Mucius."

"It is all *my* fault, noble master," Udo broke in.

Xantippus was more astonished than ever. "What? All at once the fellow can speak?" he said.

"He only pretended to be mute out of fear," said Julius hastily.

"And he even speaks an excellent Latin," Xantippus added a little more mildly. He surveyed Udo with curiosity. "Mucius," he said, "why do you think that possibly you're preventing a heinous crime?"

"Master Xanthos," Flavius cried. "We're afraid one of our fathers is going to be murdered."

Xantippus's eyes widened in surprise. "What? Why? What are you saying?"

"All of our lives are in danger," Rufus said.

"Yours, too, Master Xanthos," Antonius said. "Once the ex-gladiator finds out who we are, he might break in on us in school and kill you, too, at the same time."

"Curb your loose tongue," Xantippus said. "Your imagination is carrying you away again." Even so, he looked at the boys rather uneasily. "Mucius, tell me here and now, what is this all about?"

"I'm sorry, Master Xanthos," Mucius said. "The story is hard to believe, and everything is still swirling around in my head."

"Pull yourself together," said Xantippus. "After all, you want to be a great orator someday. Till now you've always been halfway decent in the essay. Order your thoughts! Cato, the famous statesman, has said: 'Master the material, the words will follow.' "

"That's just it, Master Xanthos, the material is so complicated that I don't know where to start." Mucius went on to tell a somewhat rambling story of Udo's adventure at the cemetery, his flight through the city, and his encounter with the drunken gladiators who sold him to Callon. Finally, he explained about the letter in the cloak that Udo had left lying in a cellar somewhere.

Xantippus remained silent. He stroked his pointed beard thoughtfully.

"I wanted to warn our fathers," Flavius said.

"I'm against it, Master Xanthos," Julius said. "There are nine hundred senators in the Senate. Why should it coincidentally be one of our fathers who's threatened?"

"My dear students, let's think logically," Xantippus said with concern.

The boys were happy. Xantippus was sensible and seemed to want to help them.

"At the moment there are eight hundred and seventy-six senators in the Senate," he went on. "Of those, only twenty-five or thirty are famous. All the others, in my view anyway, are superfluous. Unfortunately, our honored Emperor has deemed it necessary to pack the Senate with his pitiful favorites—among them, nauseating play-actors, bloodthirsty gladiators, and, from what I've heard, he even made one of his cooks a senator."

The boys instinctively looked over at the entrance in fear—had anybody happened to overhear what Xantippus was saying, their tutor now would be as good as dead.

Xantippus resumed without a qualm. "Of the twenty-five or thirty famous senators, half are famous only for having killed other senators."

Antonius piped up, "My father even knew two senators who killed each other in an argument over where to hang their cloaks in the Senate corridor."

"Quiet," Xantippus commanded. "Therefore, that leaves just fifteen senators who rightly can be called famous, and your fathers are numbered among them.

According to the mathematical laws of probability, the numerical proportion is one to one, and the chance that one of your fathers is meant is high. Do you understand all this?"

"I'm afraid so," Julius said with a sigh.

8

He Must Smell of Mimosa

"Now listen closely," Xantippus said. "Let's think systematically, my dear students. First, before Pollino arrives in Rome, we must find the letter. That's an axiom."

"An axiom? What's that?" Flavius asked.

"An axiom is a principle that is immediately evident and needs no proof. You should really know that by now."

"I just forgot."

"I hope you still remember Euclid."

The boys wondered what Euclid might have to do with the letter.

"I know who Euclid is," said Antonius, raising his hand. "He's the man who invented the shortest line between two points."

His friends laughed. Udo did, too.

"Quiet!" Xantippus thundered. "Antonius, is that supposed to be funny perhaps?"

"Certainly not!" Antonius said, beaming. "The man meant it seriously."

Xantippus sighed. "Euclid was the greatest mathematician of Greece. In his famous *Elements of Geometry* he established that there is only a single straight line between two points. That is an axiom."

The boys didn't understand how a straight line could help them.

"Master Xanthos," Julius said, "I'm afraid Udo hasn't the faintest idea of what cellar the cloak is lying in. It's hopeless to think of finding the letter."

"A man who no longer hopes no longer lives," Xantippus said. "Just as a dead tree cannot bring forth new leaves. Udo," he said, "come over here and sit there, across from me."

Udo jumped up and sat on a crate at Xantippus's feet. He looked at him expectantly.

"Swear by all your gods that you have told the truth and nothing but the truth!"

"I swear by all my gods that I have told the truth and nothing but the truth," Udo said.

Xantippus nodded. "Now, my son, you say you have been Pollino's personal slave. Do you have any hint of who's to be murdered?"

"No, noble master."

"Did you ever happen to hear why your lord wanted to have a famous senator put out of the way?"

"Once I heard fragments of a conversation that could have had some connection with the assassination plot," Udo said. "About two months ago a man came to visit my lord. Over dinner they were talking in a strange way. It struck me that they fell silent every time I came in to serve them. But I did pick up a few scraps of conversation—though only outside the door," he admitted, smiling. "Once my lord said, 'There's just one man who could be dangerous to us—he's said to be a famous senator. My spies still don't know who he is, but they're on the scent. He absolutely must be done away with or else we're not safe.' My lord also spoke of a cage he was having transported to Rome."

"A cage?" Xantippus was astonished.

"I know what cage he was speaking about. In the cage was a wild bear, a gift from my lord to the zoological gardens in Rome. I was there when the cage was lifted onto the wagon by twenty-four legionnaires. There were twelve draft oxen in harness to pull it."

"Twenty-four legionnaires and twelve draft oxen!" Antonius cried. "That can't have been a bear. It was a mammoth."

"Quiet!" Xantippus said.

"Then, too, I heard my lord and the man frequently mention General Varus and the Teutoburg

Forest. What that has to do with the plan to murder
a senator is a riddle to me."

"To me also," Xantippus said. "Of course there
are a great many wild bears in Germania. But there

was only one Varus, and he is dead." He looked at his students. "Attention! What do you know about Varus, eh?"

"Varus?" Antonius said. "I don't know him."

"Never heard of him," Publius put in.

Varus seemed to be an unknown celebrity to the others, too.

"Very sad, very sad," Xantippus said. "It's about time I refreshed your knowledge of history a bit. Eleven years ago Augustus, the dead Emperor, sent Varus along with three of his best legions to Germania to put down a revolt. Unfortunately, the Germans turned the tables. Under the leadership of their national hero, Hermann, they attacked Varus and his legionnaires in the Teutoburg Forest and beat him so badly only a handful of legionnaires escaped. Varus himself committed suicide. It was one of the most catastrophic defeats the Roman Empire has suffered.

"When Emperor Augustus heard the news, he is supposed to have collapsed in tears and lamented for days, 'Varus, Varus, give me back my legions.' I imagine the loss of the three banners with the Roman eagle and the military cashbox Varus had with him hurt the most. There were supposed to have been a hundred thousand gold pieces in it— pay for the legionnaires. That's ten million sesterces. They still haven't been found. Caius!" Xantippus shouted. "Are you listening, or are you asleep?"

Caius started from his seat. "No," he said. "I'm wide awake."

"All right, then repeat! What did Emperor Augustus cry out when he heard of Varus's defeat?"

"Augustus? Augustus?" Caius stammered. "Oh, I've got it. He is supposed to have constantly mumbled to himself, 'Varus, Varus, give me back my millions.' "

The others rocked with laughter, including Udo. Even Xantippus snickered. "Caius, you're hopeless," he said. Then he grew serious. "Quiet, please!" he said. "Unfortunately, the motive for the planned assassination remains as dark as the Teutoburg Forest—though something is dawning on me that I must first think through logically. What we must pursue with all our energy is finding the letter. The motive won't be of any help to the man who's murdered. What we need to find is the cellar where Udo's cloak is lying."

He turned to Udo. "You said that when you were running away from the cemetery in Via Salaris, you flew through many narrow and winding streets. Right?"

"Yes, noble master."

"Were the streets lined on both sides with houses?"

"Yes. I wasn't able to see at night, but the next morning, when I was fleeing from the woman who took a swing at me with her broom, I ran past nothing but tall buildings."

"The buildings were brick, were they not?"

"That's right, noble master. They were so tall, I was amazed. Many must have been at least seven stories high. I didn't know there were such high buildings anywhere."

"Good," Xantippus said. "Those are the new apartment buildings in the district between the Viminal and Quirinal hills. I think already we're getting closer to the answers to our questions."

"Excuse me, Master Xanthos," Mucius said. "I happen to be familiar with the area. It's loaded with new apartment buildings there. How can we expect to find the cellar of a definite building? Rome's smallest streets don't have a name or a number—worse luck!"

"Maybe you'd prefer we wait till a good-natured god comes along to lead you there by the nose, eh?" Xantippus said.

As a precaution, Mucius didn't say anything.

"My dear boy, I have preached to you often enough that the gods gladly bestow their favors upon him who helps himself. And I'm around to see that we help ourselves. So kindly don't interrupt me again."

He turned back to Udo. "Now think carefully. Did you fall asleep as soon as you lay down in the cellar?"

"No, noble lord. I was too excited. I listened for a while to make sure no one would come and take me off guard."

"Excellent," Xantippus said.

"I heard horses neighing in the night, also a grinding noise, as of two stones being rubbed against each other."

"Any other sounds?"

"Directly above me I kept hearing the clang of metal. It sounded like swords striking together, and a man was shouting in a rasping voice, 'Hail, Emperor! We, about to die, salute you.' "

Xantippus raised his brows in wonder. This answer from the young slave Udo seemed to confuse him. He was silent for a while, deep in thought. Suddenly he smiled. "Very probably . . . very probably . . . that must be it!" he said mysteriously. "Udo, you smelled a strong scent of mimosa, did you not?"

Udo was dumbfounded. "Noble master, how do you know that?" He stared at Xantippus as a child stares at a magician. "I actually did smell mimosa. Yes, the odor was so strong that it almost made me sick."

"Very gratifying. Magnificent!" Xantippus said. He rapped his cane with gusto on the crate where Udo was sitting and shouted, "Young men, go get the cloak and the letter without delay. It's in the cellar of a gladiator school opposite a soap factory. The building is in the third side street that runs from Long Street to Semita Street."

The boys were flabbergasted.

9

About Clanging Swords and Grindstones

"How did you figure out where the cellar is, Master Xanthos?" Flavius asked almost with reverence.

"Udo has the gift of observation," Xantippus said. "He gave me two valuable leads. You remember, I hope, that with an irregular triangle, if you know the size of two angles, you also know the size of the third."

The boys nodded. Triangles were Xantippus's favorite theme.

"Aiding me as well was the fact that I know Rome and its environs thoroughly." He pointed his cane at a corner of the cave. "I see your schoolwork flung over there in that filthy corner. Bring me a piece of chalk right away."

Antonius jumped up and brought Xantippus some chalk. He handed it over reluctantly; he preferred saving it to beautify several garden walls with his name on the way home.

"Now pay attention," Xantippus said. He stepped up to a smooth bit of the rock wall and scratched an "M" on it with the chalk. "The 'M' here is the second milestone in the Via Salaris. It's right beside the Porta Salaris. Porta Salaris is the big open gate Udo told about. There is no other gate there. Right behind it the cemetery begins."

Xantippus wrote a "C" on the wall, then drew a huge circle around the "C." "The cemetery is surrounded on the north, east, and south by sparsely populated fields. Thus, on his flight Udo could have run only to the southwest, and that means down Long Street in that quarter of the city where the tall new apartment buildings begin. I was there last month and looked around. They're located between the Viminal and Quirinal hills. Now, to the noises Udo heard. Close by he heard horses neighing, and he heard a grinding sound, too. That's the famous mill in the area. The millstones are pulled by horses, thus the neighing. Now I know, as well, that the house with the cellar he slept in must be near the mill. The question remains: Is the house *before* or *after* the mill when you're coming from Long Street? That's why I asked him about the smell of mimosa, because the building before the mill lies right across from a soap factory. It belongs to Menellis, the freed slave. He got rich by putting out a soap that smells like mimosa for women's delicate skin. Udo says he almost got sick from the odor. You see, the wind came out of the west last night and blew the odor of mimosa directly into the cellar of the house across the street."

Julius made himself heard. "Excuse me, Master Xanthos, but how do you know where the wind was coming from in the middle of the night?"

"Because I had to get up in the middle of the night to make the window hangings stop flapping. It's a west window; that's how I know where the wind was coming from. Are you satisfied?"

"Certainly, certainly, Master Xanthos."

"I'm glad."

"What was the meaning of the clanging swords Udo heard? And the shout, 'Hail, Emperor! We, about to die, salute you'?" Mucius asked.

"That did stop me a minute," Xantippus admitted. "There was only one solution. Above the cellar is a school for gladiators. Several gladiators were practicing sword fighting, and some were trying to memorize 'Hail, Emperor! We, about to die, salute you.' Gladiators may be looked upon as heroes, but not as intellectual giants. Following tradition, at the start of every match in the arena, they have to honor the Emperor by walking up to his box and shouting, 'Hail, Emperor! We, about to die, salute you.' "

"There's only one thing I don't understand, Master Xanthos," Publius said. "How could Udo hear all these noises? Isn't everybody sleeping at midnight?"

"No doubt you are," Xantippus grumbled. "You even sleep at your classes during the day. All the slaves in the factory begin work at midnight. All right, now stop your questions. On your feet and get the letter. If the gods have been merciful, in the meantime maybe nobody has found the cloak."

"I don't think they have, noble master," Udo spoke up. "The cloak is well hidden in a corner behind two barrels."

"Once you have the letter, come immediately to my apartment," Xantippus told his pupils. "Come even if you don't have it."

"May we open it if we find it?" Julius asked.

"No. I want to study the seal carefully first, to assure its authenticity."

"What should we do with Udo meanwhile?" Rufus asked.

"Leave him here. We may need him yet. Bring him something to eat first before you come to see

me." Xantippus went to the doorway. "By the way,
I will be passing the Arch of Triumph of Augustus
and will pay the vendor for the honey. He shouldn't
be out of pocket. I will then tell you what I paid for
it." He tossed Antonius's chalk on a crate, breaking
it into many tiny pieces; then he disappeared.

"My chalk. What a dirty trick!" Antonius wailed.

"The honey can cost us a bar of gold." Julius
sighed.

"Maybe we can pay off Xantippus in installments," Flavius suggested.

"Xantippus is the wrong shop for that," Publius said with a sneer. He was mad because Xantippus had berated him.

"Get a move on," Mucius ordered. "To Long Street."

10

"Hail, Emperor! We, About to Die, Salute You!"

At the Forum the boys kept behind the pillars of the basilica and looked in all directions to make sure the ex-gladiator didn't surprise them again.

"I hope that monster isn't lying in wait for us somewhere," Flavius said.

"He has other things to do," Publius said, smirking. "It will take him hours to get rid of that honey."

Before the Senate building a herald announced so loudly that his call resounded across the square, "The shadow of the sun has reached the line at my feet—the noon hour has come!"

The Forum, swarming with people, emptied quickly. Many went home to sleep, but most hurried to their favorite bathhouses or swimming halls, of which there were almost two hundred in Rome. The operators of the countless stands and vending carts around packed up their wares—ugly souvenirs usually purchased just by foreigners, and other cheap knickknacks. Then they closed the shutters of their shops to take a long nap. The more fashionable stores on the side streets closed for the day soon afterward.

Only the senators in the Senate had to keep going. By order of the Emperor they were not allowed to leave until the proposal for raising taxes had been voted on.

Perhaps they were not unhappy about that, though, for it was cool in the Senate, while outdoors the sun burned down on the city. The pavement under the boys' sandals felt red-hot to them.

Once on Long Street at last, they were able to walk in the shadow of the Viminal Hill. When they turned the corner at the third street, they saw the tall apartment buildings and also got their first sniff of mimosa. The farther they went, the more stupefying was the smell, so they could not possibly miss the soap factory. Three leaden smokestacks busily poured out clouds of smoke. Behind the palings of the loading platform, slaves filled up crates with boxes of soap.

Diagonally across from the factory lay the mill Xantippus spoke of. The boys heard horses snorting, whips cracking, and the millstones grinding.

Mucius studied the houses on the other side attentively. On the sidewalks in front were mounds of filth. Garbage was piled up everywhere, and amidst it all were discarded pieces of broken furniture. Ragged little children played with noisy hilarity on the roadway, which didn't look much cleaner. The boys tossed leather balls to each other; the girls played skip rope. Others wore wreaths of flowers on their heads and danced round dances.

Almost all of the houses had balconies decorated with flower boxes that were overflowing with geraniums or petunias. They stood out conspicuously against the signs of ruin all about them. Lines were strung from house to house, crisscrossing and hung with colorful laundry that flapped in the wind.

Two women were leaning out their windows and staring curiously at the well-dressed boys down on the street. Directly above them a woman dumped a pail of rinse water out, and they had to duck inside quickly to avoid getting splashed.

"I don't like it here," Flavius said.

"We're not here to have a good time," Mucius said. "Julius, can you see a cellar entrance in the house to the right of the mill?"

"No, there's only a milk store and a butcher. Between them is a small workshop, though. The door is open."

"There isn't a gladiator school anywhere around," Rufus said.

"Xantippus has made a fool of himself," Publius said. "So he isn't perfect, either."

"We'd better not shoot the bow behind the arrow," Mucius said. "Maybe it's the house to the left of the mill."

They walked over but found no cellar entrance there and returned, disappointed, to the first house. They stood around for a while uncertain of what to do. They were almost ready to give up and leave when they suddenly listened, spellbound. From the workshop came the sound of clanging swords, and somebody yelled stridently, "Hail, Emperor! We, about to die, salute you!"

Mucius ran over and looked in the workshop. The others followed and peered over his shoulders. A man with his back turned to them was standing in front of an anvil and pounding a huge hammer on a bent sword—he must be a smith who repaired swords.

"Hail, Emperor! We, about to die, salute you!" was shrieked again. Mucius broke into a laugh. A cage hung from the ceiling, and in it a parrot was hopping excitedly back and forth on its perch. It was gaping at the boys with its head bent and crying repeatedly, "Hail, Emperor! We, about to die, salute you!"

"A parrot . . ." Flavius said. "Who would have imagined?"

"And there are the stairs to the cellar, too," Antonius burst out.

Now the others saw, too. Just inside the workshop, to the right of the entrance, was a stairway leading to a cellar.

"Udo must have run down there when the smith happened to be out," Julius said.

The boys stared uneasily at the man's broad back. He looked as big and strong as the maniac who had attacked them in the Forum. Maybe the smith was an ex-gladiator, too, and his friends had him fix their swords. And it was probably from them that the parrot had learned the solemn salute to the Emperor.

"How are we going to get the cloak now?" Julius whispered, looking with dread at the smith.

"You stay here at the door," Mucius said in an undertone. "You must cover my retreat. I'll sneak down to the cellar, and if I'm lucky, the man won't notice." He lost no time but set off on tiptoe into the depths, bent on his mission.

While he was gone, his friends held their breaths and didn't let the smith out of their sight. Mucius emerged nimbly, swinging Udo's rolled-up cloak in his hand with a triumphant flourish.

At this moment a woman with a broom in her hand came in through the back door. She caught sight of Mucius and bawled out, "Hey, Emos, help! That's the thief from last night."

She pounced on Mucius like a tigress teased into madness and swung her broom handle over his head.

The smith turned with a baffled look and just stood beside his anvil as if rooted there.

Mucius hurtled outside to his friends, the woman with the broom at his heels. "Stop the thief!" she screamed.

"Hail, Emperor! We, about to die, salute you!" the parrot shrieked.

"Quick . . . quick, Mucius," his friends cried. They raced down the street with him—almost running over a throng of children—tore around the corner of Long Street, and kept on running until they ran out of breath.

They ducked behind a wall of the Baths of Constantine and peered around the corner to make sure they weren't being pursued.

"No one's in sight," Rufus said.

Mucius rubbed his forehead. "Now I've caught a good one from the broom like Udo did," he said. "That's going to make a beautiful lump."

"It doesn't matter," Publius said. "The main thing is you've got the cloak."

"Give me the letter," Caius said.

Mucius kneeled down, rolled open the cloak, and dug into the right-hand pocket. He produced a money purse. "All that's in this pocket is Udo's money," he muttered. He reached into the other pocket and pulled his hand out empty. "There's no letter in the cloak," he said, and looked at the others as if all were lost.

Now We're Back Where
We Started

Xantippus was examining Udo's cloak, which he had spread out in front of him while he carefully searched the lining.

The boys had stormed in on him excitedly, like the Greeks into the Trojan fortress, and thrown the cloak on the table. Now they waited impatiently to hear what he would say in his disappointment at the missing letter.

Xantippus had been sitting at the desk in his study a little while before.

"A sad turn of affairs this is . . . no letter, after all," Xantippus said. He fell silent and scratched his beard thoughtfully.

Outdoors, the district fire brigade clattered past, clanging shrilly. There was a fire every day somewhere in Rome. No one ever got very excited about them except those whose houses were going up in flames. The clanging faded in the distance. A moment later the hurried clicking of the hobnailed boots of policemen could be heard on the pavement; the Guard troops were probably running behind the fire brigade.

The boys didn't look out the window once. "Udo has been deceiving all of us," Caius said. Caius hadn't liked slaves ever since one had put a frog in his bed and another had leaped at him with a devil's mask on his face. Of course, those things had been done on All Fools' Day, which was celebrated every year at the end of December.

"Nonsense," Xantippus said. "Udo hasn't lied. You did find the cloak, didn't you? It's more likely that Udo, without knowing it, lost the letter when he was running away. Publius, from what I've heard, you're a famous runner. Run to the cave and bring Udo here. I must speak to him."

"Master Xanthos," Julius said, "it's better for Udo not to be seen. Maybe the ex-gladiator is looking everywhere for him."

"We could carry Udo in a sedan chair," Antonius suggested. "There are all kinds of chairs for rent at Aemilius Bridge. It's a lot cheaper if you carry them yourself."

"That will take too long," Xantippus said. He

stood up, his mind obviously closed. "We'll go to Udo," he said. "Get me my stick."

The boys scattered and looked everywhere for the stick, but their efforts were unnecessary. The hanging between the schoolroom and Xantippus's apartment was pushed aside, and a strange creature knocked on the archway. The creature had a rag wrapped around his head. Only his nose was exposed.

"May I come in, noble master?" the creature asked.

"Udo . . ." the boys cried in surprise.

"Come in, Udo," Xantippus said. "Your arrival is like the answer to a call."

Udo tore off the rag. "I put this thick cloth over my head so I wouldn't be recognized on the way," he explained. "It wasn't exactly pleasant in the heat, but I prefer the warmth of life to the cold of Hades."

"Udo," Mucius said sternly, "we couldn't find a letter in your cloak."

"That's why I came here, young master," Udo said. "You mentioned that you were going to bring me some food before coming here with the cloak. Then I would have shown you where the letter was."

"The letter *is* in the cloak?" Rufus said.

"It's sewn into the collar. And it's not written

on papyrus, but on linen so that it can't be felt
through the lining."

"Oh, that's it . . ." Xantippus grumbled, and
he coughed. He seemed to be somewhat annoyed
that he himself hadn't hit upon the idea. "Flavius,
go get a knife from the kitchen."

Flavius dashed out of the room.

"Why did you sew the letter on the inside?" Julius asked.

"It's a long journey from the Rhine to the Tiber, young master. If I'd lost the letter, I would have been lost myself. Of course, I didn't suspect at the time that I was carrying around my own death warrant."

"Good," Xantippus said. "Now go to the kitchen and get yourself something from the pantry to eat. You must be hungry."

"Thank you," Udo said. Suddenly enlivened, he rushed into the kitchen.

"I'm starved, too," Caius said.

"Me, too," said Publius.

"You can eat at home afterward," Xantippus said. "I'm not running an inn here. Udo has no home."

"I don't want anything to eat before I know what's in the letter," Mucius said.

"That's right," Julius and Antonius agreed.

Xantippus didn't allow matters to rush ahead so swiftly, however. He placed the letter on the table and first studied it from the outside. "It's folded into a perfect square," he said with satisfaction. "First of all, I have to check the seal." He produced a round, polished emerald out of a drawer, stuck it in his right eye, and bent over the letter. "The seal is genuine," he announced after a while. "I recognize the Pollino family's coat of arms: an eagle with two crossed swords beneath it."

"That's the brand on Udo's arm, too," Antonius called out.

Xantippus broke the seal and unfolded the letter. He placed the emerald in the drawer and closed it.

All this time the boys were bursting with curiosity. By Pluto, they wanted finally to hear whom the conspirators wanted dead.

Xantippus read the letter to himself, then he looked up. "No name of a famous senator who is supposed to be murdered is mentioned in the letter," he said. "I will read it to you."

"Dear Friend:

Go to the Viminal. Across from the statue of Niobe lies the villa in which Cicero lived.

Usipetes

Don't forget, dear friend, before you set off, start at the Temple of Castor and Pollux."

Xantippus dropped the letter. "That's all it says."

"Great Jupiter," Mucius moaned, "now we're back where we started."

12

Caius Sees the Light

"We'll never find out which of our fathers is supposed to be murdered," Julius said.

Flavius replied with excitement, "Yet it's all there clearly, in the letter, who is meant."

"Is that so?" Xantippus said with a drawl. "Maybe after all you're more intelligent than I've given you credit for up to now, my friend."

"It's Cicero," Flavius said. "Cicero is the most famous senator of all, isn't he?"

Xantippus sighed. "Unfortunately, Cicero was killed seventy-one years ago at the instigation of Marcus Antonius, Flavius. I hope you realize it would be wasted effort to kill him again. Correct?"

Flavius fell silent in shame.

"Master Xanthos," Mucius said, "shouldn't we call Udo in to tell us in detail once more what he heard at the cemetery? Couldn't that somehow help us?"

"No. 'He who wants to advance cannot look backward,' " Xantippus quoted. "We're not going to let hope fade away so easily, my dear pupils. The following has occurred to me: The contents of the letter are apparently harmless so that in case it should fall into the wrong hands, nothing would be revealed. But the contents make no sense. There's neither a statue of Niobe on the Viminal, nor a villa where Cicero supposedly lived. I ask myself: Why did Pollino choose these particular names? I would swear they are some sort of secret code known by the conspirators here in Rome. If we could break the code, we would discover the name of the famous senator."

Udo returned from the kitchen in silence and sat down modestly on a stool in the background.

"Let's consider these names a little more closely," Xantippus resumed.

"The first name is Viminal. At the moment this tells us nothing. Viminal is one of the seven hills on which the city of Rome is built. Number two is Niobe. Julius, who was Niobe?"

Julius stood up and started reeling off what he knew. "Niobe was the myth about the Queen of Thebes. She was the daughter of Tantalus. Tantalus was the man who was consigned for all eternity to roll a rock up a hill, and it always rolled back again."

"Shame on you, Julius," Xantippus interrupted. "Again you've confused Tantalus with Sisyphus. Won't you ever get that right? It wasn't Tantalus but Sisyphus who slaved with the rock. On the other hand, Tantalus was the poor unfortunate who was condemned to the torment of eternal hunger and thirst. Sit down, Julius. Anyhow, a few fragments of Greek mythology have stuck in your head. Let's pursue the idea of Niobe a little further. Maybe that will give us a hint regarding the code. Now, Niobe wasn't exactly very happy. The god Apollo and the goddess Diana cruelly murdered Niobe's fourteen children in the presence of their mother. As if that weren't enough, Zeus turned her into a statue. But that didn't stop her from crying over the death of her children. We'll have to keep this tragic story in mind. Name number three—Cicero. Explanation superfluous. Every schoolboy knows who Cicero is and when he lived—except for the pupil Flavius. The letter is signed with the name Usipetes. I must admit to never having heard this word."

Udo threw his hand up and came forward as though he, too, were one of Xantippus's pupils.

"Speak, Udo," Xantippus said, nodding to encourage him. Udo seemed to be an educated young man.

"Usipetes is a German tribe living on the right shore of the Rhine," he said. "I come from a region lying on the left shore. Previously, we often attacked the other side, but in the last few years we've made peace and are good friends. They celebrate our holidays with us, and we ours with them. We provide casks full of wine; their beer flows in streams."

"Thank you," Xantippus said amiably. "One never learns except through living. The names we still have left are Castor and Pollux, the inseparable twins. They are sons of Zeus and are thought of as Rome's protectors. What can those two divine twins offer us?

"Not much, I'm afraid. Castor buried himself in raising wild horses, while his twin brother Pollux devoted himself to the questionable art of boxing. So, now we've run through all the names once. Rufus, get a slate and a piece of chalk out of the schoolroom."

Rufus disappeared beyond the hanging and quickly returned with the slate and chalk.

Xantippus hung the slate over a picture, and with a schoolmaster's thoroughness—which in this case he deeply regretted later—he wrote on the slate as though he were treating a mathematical problem:

In Pollino's letter, brought by Udo the messenger, the following names occur:

Viminal
Niobe
Cicero
Usipetes
Castor
Pollux.

He studied the names a moment. "What do these

names mean?" he asked. "Where does the key to the code lie?" He turned around and looked at his pupils. "The answer is—we have no idea."

Caius suddenly jumped up from his seat, in his excitement knocking over his stool. "I . . . I know who they mean," he finally got out hoarsely, almost choking.

"Hear, hear! Caius sees the light!" Publius cried scornfully.

"All right, Caius, what do you think you know?" Xantippus asked.

Caius, pale and terrified, stammered, "I . . . I . . . I know. It's *my* father who is supposed to be murdered."

13

Will the City Prefect Call Out His Whole Police Force?

The boys were astonished and stared skeptically at Caius. It was unbelievable that of all people he—whose brain usually worked so slowly—should have solved the code of the letter when it stumped even Xantippus.

"Well, Caius, tell us more," Xantippus said. "We'd like to know how you solved the riddle of the letter."

"I probably never would have solved it if it hadn't been *my* father who is in danger," Caius said excitedly. "The gods must have been smiling down on me."

"I understand," Xantippus said. "You mean, because it is *your* father, you somehow developed a sixth sense?"

"You've certainly made a mistake," Rufus said.

"I know nothing about a sixth sense," Caius said. "But I'll prove to you that this is no mistake."

He ran to the slate, grabbed the chalk, and underlined the first letter of the first four names Xantippus had written down.

"Look!" he said brightly, and pointed the chalk at the four names:

<u>V</u>iminal
<u>N</u>iobe
<u>C</u>icero
<u>U</u>sipetes
Castor
Pollux.

Then Caius read off the underlined letters aloud: "V, N, C, U. It struck me that these letters occur also in my father's name," he said.

Next he wrote on the slate, underlining the V, the N, the C, and the U:

<u>V</u> i <u>n</u> i <u>c</u> i <u>u</u> s.

"That can't be just a coincidence," he said.

Publius, laughing sarcastically, said, "But there are six names in the letter, my friend. What about the 'C' in Castor and the 'P' in Pollux?"

Caius snorted. "I didn't overlook a thing, you

ass," he said. "I was confused for a moment by Castor and Pollux, too. Like a miracle, though, suddenly I got it."

Antonius snickered.

"Quiet," said Xantippus. "Go ahead, Caius."

"In the letter there is a postscript saying: 'Start at the Temple of Castor and Pollux.' Like a bolt from the blue I got the idea. Castor and Pollux are the inseparable twins, aren't they? Pollino's intention was to remind the conspirator always to read the first two letters of the four names together."

Again he put the four first names on the slate, this time separating the first two letters from the rest:

Vi minal
Ni obe
Ci cero
Us ipetes.

He cried, "Now do you see? These eight letters, read from top to bottom, become my father's name—Vinicius."

His friends just sat there with their mouths open in awe. Even Xantippus's eyes bulged. "By all the gods," he muttered, "Caius is right."

The boys, delighted that Caius had solved the code, applauded. Udo clapped loudest of all. Caius accepted these accolades beaming, as though he were being crowned with laurel at the Olympic games.

"Caius," a pleased Xantippus said, "till now there were seven wonders in the world. Now there are eight, and you are the eighth." He turned to the other boys. "By the way, which of you can name those Seven Wonders of the World?"

Mucius jumped up. "The Seven Wonders of the World are as follows," he asserted confidently, and he went through them without a pause. "The pyramids, the Hanging Gardens of Babylon, the Temple of Diana in Ephesus, Phidias' statue of Zeus, the tomb of King Mausolus at Halicarnassus, and the Colossus at Rhodes." Proudly he sat down.

Xantippus looked at him disapprovingly. "You, my best student, disappoint me," he said.

"Why?"

"Because, unfortunately, you must not be able to count. You listed only six wonders and forgot the seventh, the lighthouse on Pharos."

Caius was listening to all this with mounting impatience. "The Seven Wonders of the World won't help me save my father, Master Xanthos," he said in anger.

"Slowly but surely, Caius," Xantippus replied. "Rome wasn't built in a day, either. As of now we've done everything possible that was to be done. Most important, we found the letter, didn't we? Without the letter you never would have discovered that the man in danger is your father. Luckily for us, the conspirators don't have the letter and still don't know that your father is supposed to be disposed of. So we can wait until he leaves the Senate. Then we'll go up to him on the spot and warn him."

"By then maybe it will be too late," Caius said. "I won't wait any longer. I'll run home, get my father's private secretary, and we'll go straight to the city prefect, Lucius Terrentius Manilius. He'll call out his whole police force."

"Don't do that!" Mucius cried. "They'll arrest Udo. You know what will happen to him then."

"My father is more important to me than a slave," Caius said. He snatched the letter from the desk and vanished through the door like a shot hurtled from a catapult.

"Caius has gone crazy again," Mucius cried.

"Should we run after him and bring him back, Master Xanthos?" Publius asked.

"No, he has every right to try anything he wants in an attempt to save his father."

"Are you saying that you don't care whether Udo is questioned by the police?" Julius asked.

"I didn't say that," Xantippus snapped. "Udo can stay here. I have a secret room next door where all my works on mathematics are kept so they won't be stolen. There's room enough to set up a bed. Udo can hide there until the danger is past."

"I thank you with all my heart, noble master," Udo said. "All the same, it would be better if the young master didn't go to the prefect."

"Why not?" Xantippus asked.

"Because by doing that, he would be delivering his father into the conspirators' hands."

"What do you mean?"

"The prefect is the man who engaged my master in that secret conversation a few months ago."

"Explain what you mean by that," said Xantippus sharply.

"I have just heard his name again from Caius," said Udo. "My master's adjutant announced the man's arrival at that time with the words: 'General, here comes the honorable Lucius Terrentius Manilius.'"

Xantippus groaned. "This gang of conspirators is like the nine-headed snake Hydra," he said. "The more heads cut off, the more grow in their places." He pounded on his desk fiercely. "Boys, attention," he said. "Run to Caius, as fast as you can. Use any means you can find to stop him from seeing the prefect. If the letter falls into the hands of Manilius, he'll not only know which famous senator he's supposed to kill, he'll also murder Caius and the secretary so they can't warn Vinicius. Hurry! Move! Then return here immediately and tell me what's happened."

14

The Boys Have No Time to Dive into the Water

The Villa Vinicius lay in the shade-softened Minerva Square on the Esquiline Hill. Mucius pounded the iron hoop door knocker against the gate. "Open quickly, please," he shouted, gasping for breath.

For the third time today the boys had run through Rome as though their lives depended on it.

Inside the gate a hinged plate was lifted, and the doorman peered through the peephole. He recognized the boys and immediately swung open the door. "May the gods attend you, noble young lords," he said in greeting. His young mistress, Claudia, had given him strict orders to admit her brother Caius's friends always and to welcome them with honors. "If I may say, the right foot forward," he urged them amiably. It was considered bad luck for anybody to step into a house with his left foot first.

"We must speak to Caius immediately," Mucius said.

"I haven't seen him today, young master," the doorman said. "But I'll tell my mistress you are here. She's just come back from the city."

Several slaves stood in the background. The doorman signaled to one of them, and he disappeared quickly behind the hanging curtain in the vestibule.

The boys brushed off their sandals and waited impatiently for his return.

"Caius must have taken a detour or else he'd be here by now," Julius said.

"Maybe he couldn't control his appetite, and he made a quick stop for some roasted chestnuts on the steps of the Capitol," Publius suggested. "He's certainly said often enough that he was hungry."

"He was far too upset to think about food," Rufus said. "Something's wrong."

The slave reappeared, holding the hanging to one side. "My mistress has asked you to come in and to be patient a moment more," he said.

The boys looked around the great hall for any sign of Caius. Oriental carpets were everywhere, even around a pool with a cheerful fountain bubbling in the center. Silver lamps, shielded with bell-shaped globes made of the finest Alexandrian glass, stood on four marble tables. Running along on the left and right were colonnades, behind which one could see the shimmer of ivory-inlaid doors leading to other rooms. The walls between were brightly painted, the murals on them depicting famous warriors out of the Roman sagas.

The slanting rays of the setting sun shone through the square opening in the ceiling and fell upon the house altar that sat within a niche in a prominent place. It was surrounded by the tutelary gods of the family. Above it colored wax masks of Vinicius's ancestors looked down on the boys. As was the custom, a small eternal flame flickered in a basin hanging from a tripod.

Antonius threw himself down full length on a sofa between puffy pillows. "I'll never get up again," he said, sighing.

"My feet hurt," Flavius said. He sat down on the ledge of the fountain.

"We've certainly done our share of chasing around since this morning," Publius added.

Rufus said, "I'd like to know what's taking Claudia so long."

"If she doesn't come pretty soon, I'm going to start looking for Caius by myself," Mucius said grimly.

Just then, Claudia called out laughingly, "Here I am." She entered from the garden accompanied by two women slaves and one of her governesses, the young Greek Lysis.

Antonius and Flavius jumped to their feet. "By Juno!" Antonius cried. "Have you just come from a wedding, Claudia?"

The other boys were surprised, too. Claudia was quite festively dressed. The boys had never seen her like that before. She was wearing a white stole made of pure silk trimmed with bands of gold, and white sandals interwoven with purple lacings, whose long ends were wrapped around her ankles in a crisscross pattern. Her hair was done in the Greek style: artfully rolled curls held high on her head with a silver ribbon and sprinkled with gold powder. Enhancing the fall of curls was a mother-of-pearl comb lavishly decorated with rubies and sapphires.

A diamond ring sparkled on her left hand, and gold bracelets glistened on both arms. A chain of small hammered bronze disks hung around her neck. A fragrance of oriental perfumes rose from her. Claudia's fingernails were manicured, her toenails were lacquered red, and even her eyelashes were artificially lengthened.

Claudia had turned twelve only a short while before. Although still young, since the death of her mother she was the acknowledged mistress of the house. The boys liked her. Often, when they were younger, they had allowed her to play with them.

"Why are you all looking at me like that?" she said.

"We're overwhelmed," Publius said with a smile. "You look like Queen Cleopatra on her coronation day."

"And you smell like the soap factory of Menellis," Mucius said as a joke.

Claudia laughed. "You'll have to forgive me for being so dressed up," she said. "I have to visit my great-aunt once a month, and I've just come back. She's the Emperor's mother. She insists that I dress like a princess so that I can impress her son, the Emperor, in case he should accidentally see me."

"The sight of you would delight even the gods on Olympus," Rufus said. Everybody laughed because Rufus often spoke inordinately and at great length about Claudia.

"Well, it's wonderful to have you here," Claudia said. "We have a new swimming pool in the garden. And imagine, it has a real little waterfall. It's so hot out today; why don't you jump in and cool off?"

"Another time with pleasure," Mucius said. "But we have no time now. Where is Caius? We must talk to him immediately about a matter of vital importance."

"Caius has gone off somewhere," Claudia said. "When I came home a few minutes ago in my sedan chair, I saw him and my father's private secretary, Tiro, run out of the garden gate as though evil spirits were after them. I called them, but they were so excited they didn't hear me."

"By the powers of heaven!" Julius blurted out. "We've come too late."

"Nonsense," Mucius said. "We can intercept them if we climb down the side of the hill. Then we'll reach the city prefecture before they do. Hurry, Publius, get our sandals out of the entrance hall. We'll cut through the garden—it's closer."

Publius tore out of the room.

Claudia heard all this with astonishment. "Why is it so important to catch up with Caius?" she asked anxiously.

"We can't explain now," Julius said.

"It's a matter of life and death," Antonius said.

Claudia looked at them, terrified. "What?" she said.

Julius asked Claudia, "Who is this Tiro? Can he be trusted?"

Claudia nodded fervently. "Oh, yes. My father got rid of his former secretary and took Tiro to replace him. Tiro's not a slave . . . he's a hostage, and you know hostages are never considered slaves. Tiro is a young prince from Armenia. After the fall of Armenia, my father brought him to Rome. He treats him like a peer and a friend. Tiro is grateful to him, and he has sworn eternal loyalty. My father trusts him without reservation."

Publius returned with the sandals, and the boys slipped them on.

"Why are you in such a hurry?" Claudia asked. "Has Caius done something wrong?" They often argued, of course, but she loved him very much.

"He's about to," Publius said.

Rufus added, "He just doesn't know it."

Claudia looked from one to the other in silence. Lysis, her young Greek girl, broke in, "Young masters, there's absolutely no point in your running to the city prefecture."

"Why not?" Mucius asked.

"The prefect isn't in his office today. Because of the terrible heat, he stayed at home. Caius and Tiro are on their way to his villa. I was present when Caius told Tiro about Udo and the letter."

"Where's the prefect's villa? Please, Lysis, quickly," said Mucius. "Publius can run ahead of us and try to catch them. He runs fast as a whippet."

"I'm afraid I don't know where the villa is, young master," Lysis said sadly.

Julius beat his fist on the table. "Now we're done for," he said.

"The spirits of the underworld are throwing rocks in our way," Antonius cried.

At that moment noises were heard in the reception hall, and excited voices rang out behind the hanging. Then the drapes were flung to one side, and four slaves entered carrying a young man whom they placed on the sofa.

Claudia ran up to him. "Tiro!" she cried. "What happened?"

Painfully, Tiro pulled himself up to a half-sitting position. His forehead was bloody, and his nose was swollen. He mumbled weakly, "Mistress, we were attacked by three men."

"Where is Caius?" all the boys cried.

"They captured him and dragged him away," Tiro said.

15

The Sieve of the Danaides

Everybody in the room fell silent.

The slaves and slave girls stood attentively near the pillars and stared anxiously at their young mistress.

The fountain, like a gay brook, continued its frolicsome tinkling. In another room a canary trilled a lilting song, and from the garden outdoors could be heard the splashing of the little waterfall Claudia had mentioned. No longer was she thinking about a cool dip in the pool, however.

"Why have they dragged off my brother?" she asked, fighting to control herself.

"One of the men recognized Caius," Tiro said. "He had only one eye, and he wore a wooden sword in his belt."

"The terrible ex-gladiator!" Flavius exclaimed.

"He's the Hercules who spoke with the mysterious fat man in the cemetery," Rufus said.

Julius offered, "The other two men probably were friends of his—most likely the gladiators who sold Udo to Callon."

Mucius turned to Tiro. "Why didn't they take you, too?" he asked.

"They didn't know Caius and I were together," Tiro said.

"They attacked us in the Via Sacra, a short way from the prefect Manilius's villa. I happened to have stopped a minute; Caius went on ahead and was waiting for me on the entrance stairs. I was kneeling down to tie one of my sandal thongs that had come undone when I heard somebody shout, 'You rascal, where have you hidden the slave, Udo?' I saw three men grab Caius and drag him away. I ran to them and threw myself between them. But it was as if I had run against the walls of Jericho. One man hit me over the head with a sandbag, another punched me in the nose, and the one with one eye hurled me out in the street, where I lay half conscious a long time. When I came to, the men had vanished with Caius."

Claudia cried out, "Oh, I implore the merciful gods not to let them hurt Caius."

Lysis tried to comfort her. "All they want is to find out where Udo is, Claudia," she said. "When Caius tells them, they will let him go."

"Caius will never betray Udo," Rufus said. "Caius is a true Roman. He'd rather be murdered than endanger the life of his father."

Limp with fear, Claudia sank into an armchair. "My father's life endangered?" she said. "What are you saying?"

A slave leaped to her side and dutifully pushed a low bronze footstool under her feet. Two Arab boys fanned her with huge fronds made from ostrich feathers.

"Mucius," Claudia said. "I insist that you tell me everything that is going on."

Mucius signaled to her, indicating the slaves with a movement of his head. Not all slaves were to be trusted; many gossiped too much. Claudia understood; she sent the boy and girl slaves out of the room, permitting only Lysis, who had raised her and was more like an older sister than a governess, to remain.

Mucius told her of the conspiracy, of Udo, and about the letter. "But luck's still on our side, Claudia," he said. "The conspirators know nothing of your father."

That didn't calm Claudia, however. "My poor father." She sighed, and she began to weep.

Disconcerted, the boys were silent.

Claudia wiped her tears away with a handkerchief, rubbing her artificial eyelashes down her cheeks. "Why would anybody want to kill my father?" she asked, still sobbing.

"That's something I'm afraid we can't figure out, either," Rufus said, holding back tears himself. He was shaken by Claudia's crying.

"Tiro, you certainly must know why," Claudia said.

"No, I don't know, mistress," Tiro said. "It must involve a high secret of state, or our master would have confided it to me. I think he does have some pressing worries, though, because for some time now he has been unusually reserved, as though he were weighed down by a heavy burden."

"But what happens to my brother if he refuses to speak?" Claudia said.

Flavius tried to console her. "You mustn't immediately assume the worst," he said. "Caius will give his sacred oath that he doesn't know where Udo is. He'll swear that Udo ran away."

"I would tell them simply that Udo fell into the Tiber," Antonius said brightly. "No . . . I would say that he was transformed by a witch into a toad. There are so many toads, and how would the conspirators know which was the right one? Or . . ."

"Stop it." Mucius interrupted him. "You forget that even if, under pressure, Caius tells where Udo is, it won't be of any use to the conspirators. Xantippus has hidden Udo in a secret room. We must tell Xantippus right away so that he is warned. He himself should be hiding at a friend's or somewhere else, instead of staying at the school."

"Xantippus must disguise himself," Antonius said. "I'll get him a wig from our hairdresser. They all loan out wigs. Xantippus puts on the wig and also cuts off his beard. Then he flees to Pompeii and creeps into the crater of Vesuvius. Better yet, he could sail to Crete on the next boat and hide in the famous Labyrinth of the Minotaur. Nobody would ever find him there."

"I'm for that, too," Publius said.

"Shut up, you two," Mucius said. "Publius, why don't you race over to Xantippus now and tell him everything?"

"That's unnecessary," Julius said.

"Why?" the others exclaimed.

"The letter!" Julius blurted out. "Caius is carrying that dangerous letter. If the conspirators find it, they won't need Udo anymore. All they want to know is in the letter in black and white."

"Almighty Hercules," Mucius groaned. "I hadn't given the letter a thought."

"Vinicius is doomed," Flavius said to himself.

"And Caius, too," Rufus muttered, with a sidelong glance at Claudia.

Claudia looked from one to the other, her eyes huge with terror.

"Why should the conspirators think Caius would have the letter?" Publius said. "To them he's just a boy who happens to know Udo."

"Why? Why?" Julius mocked. "Certainly, the ex-gladiator is not so stupid as you. He caught Caius directly in front of the door to the prefect's villa. He must assume Caius got the letter from Udo so that he could show it to Manilius. That's probably why the ex-gladiator and his friends were waiting in ambush, to block his plan."

"Do you mind telling me where he would learn that Caius is Vinicius's son?" Rufus asked. "Caius doesn't have it branded on his forehead."

"What other boy would be running to the prefect's if it weren't his father in danger?" Julius replied irritably.

"You are the stupid one, not I," sneered Publius.

Julius was taken by surprise. "Why?"

"The ex-gladiator would have calmly let him go to the prefect with the letter. Manilius is one of the conspirators, remember, according to Udo's story. The prefect and Pollino are working together hand in glove."

However, Rufus was not content. "Then explain to me, Publius, why the ex-gladiator attacked and kidnapped Caius? Why didn't he let him go to see the prefect?"

"Very simple." Antonius interpreted. "The ex-gladiator recognized Caius as the boy who dumped the jug of honey over his head. He'd like nothing better than to get revenge."

"The ex-gladiator didn't even notice who dumped the honey over his head," Julius countered. "He had his back turned to Caius. No, the ex-gladiator only wants to learn from Caius where Udo is. He wants to get hold of the letter and bring it to the prefect himself, to learn whom he's supposed to kill so that finally he can earn his thousand sesterces. He seems to be very greedy."

"I'm not even trying to follow you anymore," Rufus muttered. "I'm losing my mind."

"I am, too," Flavius said. "I wish Xantippus were here. This entire affair is more futile than the Sieve of the Danaides, where no matter how much water you dip from the well, it all flows out again through the sieve."

Claudia, Tiro, and Lysis listened to the complicated arguments of Caius's friends with mounting wonder. The boys still were unable to agree.

"The holes are not in the sieve—the holes are in your heads," Mucius asserted defiantly.

"Why do you say that?" Julius asked.

"Because the ex-gladiator did take Caius prisoner out of fear that he might show the prefect the letter," Mucius went on. "The ex-gladiator doesn't have the vaguest idea that the prefect is a conspirator. Udo saw the two fellows at the cemetery, don't you remember? He told us the ex-gladiator asked the mysterious fat man who disguised his voice, 'Who are you, anyway? And who are your other chums?' "

"By Pluto, you are right," Julius cried.

Now Tiro interrupted. "Young masters," he said, "you're all proceeding from a false assumption."

"What do you mean?" the boys said.

"Caius doesn't have the letter with him at all. Before we left for the prefect's, he gave me the letter. Here it is." He pulled it out of his tunic and showed it to the boys.

"Why didn't you tell us this earlier?" Julius demanded.

"Young master," Tiro said, "has anybody ever hit you over the head with a sandbag?"

"No," Julius had honestly to admit.

"I'm only coming back to my senses slowly, and it just occurred to me that *I* have the letter. I must ask you to forgive me."

"If Caius doesn't have the letter, it may not look so bad for him, after all," Rufus said, rejoicing.

"Not at the moment," Tiro said. "But unfortunately, tomorrow or the day after, Pollino will be arriving from Germania. It's well known that he's on his way to Rome. Pollino is the one who marked our master out as his target. As luck would have it, he also knows Caius."

Claudia threw her hand to her mouth. "Oh, no," she cried. "He'll have Caius murdered so that he can't warn our father."

Helpless, the others fell silent.

"We must free Caius from that monster's claws before Pollino arrives," Rufus said at last with fierce determination.

"That's sweet of you, Rufus," Claudia said. She smiled at him in gratitude.

" 'Free Caius' is easily said," Publius suggested. "But we don't know where he is."

"He's got to be locked up somewhere in the ex-gladiator's cellar," Rufus said.

"Very smart," Julius said. "Maybe by chance you also know where the ex-gladiator lives?"

"No," Rufus confessed in shame.

"Hold your breaths, comrades," Mucius said excitedly. "I know what we must do."

The others looked at him in expectation. Rarely did Mucius propose anything stupid.

"We know from Udo that the two conspirators are supposed to meet again around midnight at the cemetery. We'll hide ourselves close by, listen, and then follow the ex-gladiator to his house. We'll wait until he falls asleep, and then we'll save Caius."

"Fantastic." Antonius cheered enthusiastically.

But Julius was disappointed. "Why should the ex-gladiator go to the cemetery again tonight? Certainly he knows that in the meantime Udo has escaped," he said.

"You're crazy," Mucius retorted. "He might know, but the mysterious fat man doesn't. The ex-gladiator has to go to the cemetery to tell the fat man about Udo. Probably about Caius, too."

"The man is a professional murderer," Tiro said. "He won't give up his thousand gold pieces so easily."

"You're right," Julius said. "The cemetery remains our last chance."

"Maybe we'll even see a ghost," Antonius said hopefully.

"Ghosts haunt your head," Publius taunted.

"Will you try to be very, very careful, too?" Claudia pleaded, deeply concerned.

"We'll hide ourselves as well as Diogenes did in his barrel," Mucius promised with a laugh.

"Oh, friends," Antonius burst out. "This will be exciting!" He rubbed his hands together in pleasure.

16

Not a Sound Passed Their Lips

Mucius, who had run on ahead to the cemetery, stopped under three sycamore trees not far from the mausoleum Udo had described, and he beckoned to his friends to join him.

Avoiding the route through the city, they had instead gone single file from the Esquiline Hill down a lonesome, narrow path along the old walls of Servius Tullius's fortress up to the huge gate at the Via Salaris. On their way they armed themselves with sticks they picked up in a clearing in case they were attacked by dogs. Their luck was good; they advanced rapidly and without incident and entered the cemetery half an hour before midnight.

Publius, Julius, Rufus, Flavius, and Antonius gathered around Mucius. He put his finger to his mouth. "Speak softly," he reminded them. "Later, when those two cutthroats get here, we'll have to be as quiet as the dead around us."

"Sometimes the dead turn over in their graves," Antonius said.

Mucius let that pass. "You know the ex-gladiator is a monster," he said. "The mysterious fat man probably is no gentle lamb, either. Just try not to breathe too heavily."

"I can hold my breath for hours," Antonius bragged.

"Then we can bury you here, too." Publius snickered.

A cock crowed in one of the small farms somewhere in the distance.

"It's a bad omen for a cock to crow at midnight," Rufus said.

Flavius already despaired of breathing the way he should. He could feel his heart beat loudly in his throat. A cemetery was no place for him.

Tiro had cleverly advised them to dress in dark capes. Claudia had provided them with six capes of brown goatskin; Caius, who was spoiled, had almost a dozen of them hanging in his wardrobe.

The full moon shone rather brightly behind a thin layer of clouds, and it bathed the cemetery in a pale light. The tombstones and monuments, whose niches held urns containing the ashes of the dead, threw grotesque shadows over the ground. Some looked like spirits of the underworld reaching out their arms to seize them.

"Pull off your sandals now," Mucius said. "We won't have time later when we start following them. We must not be heard."

"If we leave our sandals lying here, we won't find them again in the dark," Rufus protested. He didn't like giving up his sandals. They were made of the finest calfskin, a gift from Claudia for his twelfth birthday.

"We'll pick them up tomorrow," Julius said.

"That's what you say," Antonius said. "In the meantime, they will already have been stolen by twenty-five thieves."

"You don't have to leave your sandals here,"

Mucius said. "Tie the laces together and wrap them around your waist. But listen closely now. Three stone paths lead away from the mausoleum, unfortunately at a great distance apart. Since we don't know which of the three the ex-gladiator and the mysterious fat man are taking when they leave the cemetery, we're going to have to split up. Publius and you, Rufus, hide on both sides of the left path, there off to the rear. Antonius and I will take the center one. And you, Julius and Flavius, watch this path here going past the sycamores. Which of us is going to follow the two men depends on which path they choose."

"You mean, if they go by Flavius and me, we will be the ones to follow them?" Julius asked.

"That's right," Mucius said. "We others will be too far away to be able to join up with you. Besides, there are too many tombs and monuments between the paths." He had pulled off his sandals and tied them around his waist. "Are you ready?" he asked.

"Hail, Mucius! We, about to die, salute you," Publius said with a smile.

"One thing more," Mucius said. "Those who stay behind will meet in front of the mausoleum after the others follow the conspirators. Then count to a hundred and return along the fortress wall to Claudia's."

"Wait! That won't work," said Julius.

"Why not?" Mucius asked.

"We can't do this to Xantippus. He's already been waiting five hours for us to tell him what happened to Caius."

"Immortal gods," Mucius moaned. "In all the excitement I'd forgotten about Xantippus."

"He'll be waiting for us in a rage," Publius said.

"All right," Mucius said. "Instead of going to Claudia's, go first to Xantippus. Tell him everything that's happened. Whoever is doing the following should go to Xantippus's place, too, once they've carried out their mission. The others will wait for them there. Now, steal away to your posts and hide yourselves so well that nobody will be able to see you from either the paths or from the mausoleum. Again, not a sound must pass your lips!"

"I'm afraid I won't be able to hide very close to the path," Julius said. "You know there are times when my stomach growls pretty loud."

"Your stomach has no reason to growl," Mucius hissed in exasperation. "Claudia's dinner for us was more than plentiful." He gave Antonius a sign, and they disappeared. Publius and Rufus vanished, too.

Earlier, the boys had told Claudia that they hadn't eaten all day and they were starved. Claudia had called the house steward and ordered him to prepare some food.

"I'm afraid I'm in no condition to make you a proper meal in a hurry," she said, excusing herself.

"That's all right," Mucius said. "I'd even eat shoe leather."

The boys had stretched out on three divans placed around the low alabaster table. In no time, a dozen slaves hurried to them with golden platters, knives, and spoons, with silver goblets and glass bowls filled with sweet-smelling water for cleaning the fingers. A second swarm of slaves brought plates of cold meat, smoked fowl, and frogs' legs in wine sauce. There were, besides, thick slices of farm bread, heated raisin rolls, and salt sticks.

While the boys helped themselves energetically, several slaves placed jugs of Chinese porcelain on the table. Lemon juice sweetened with honey was in some of them, fresh milk from the country in others. For dessert, six Syrian boys served assorted cheeses. Then they passed around grapes, dates, apples, walnuts, and caraway biscuits.

After eating, the boys could hardly keep their eyes open. Claudia told them to lie down and sleep as they still had plenty of time before their departure.

"If we go to sleep, I won't get up again before next week," Publius said.

Claudia had to laugh in spite of her concern.

"You'll wake up in plenty of time," she said. "My father just bought one of the new water clocks. It's there, on the table. You set it for any time you wish, and it will ring so shrilly you'll fall out of bed. I'll have it set for an hour before midnight. I'll get up then, too, to wait for you to come back."

Flavius suddenly realized to his dismay that his mother would be worried if he wasn't home by midnight. This thought also had been disturbing his friends. Their mothers definitely would understand, but the boys were afraid they wouldn't be allowed to go out again once they went home. They discussed the matter. Claudia had finally proposed to send Herodus, Caius's private tutor, to tell all the mothers that their sons had been invited to a moon festival by Caius and would stay overnight in the Villa Vinicius.

The boys agreed to the idea and lay down to sleep.

Now Flavius was thinking longingly of the good food and the comfortable divan. He lay doubled up behind a tombstone on a mound of earth that was covered with pebbles. To his right, a tall fir tree towered against the night sky. In front of his face a wreath of mildewed flowers leaned against the monument. Something crawled over his legs, a spider or an ant, but he dared not move. The ground be-

neath him was damp and smelled sour. The grave
must have been filled just a short time before. Next
to him an open grave gaped like a giant black mouth.
Suddenly, a muffled screaming sounded over his
head and shook him to the marrow of his bones. He
jumped to his feet in terror and saw an owl flap
away. Taking a deep breath of relief, but still feeling
wobbly, he lay down again. His friends were no-
where in sight. He felt like a man alone in this eerie
world. The waiting time seemed to last an eternity.
A golden shower of stars swept across the heavens.
He wondered how this was possible, for, after all,

the stars were only holes in the firmament through which the divine light from the world of the gods shone through.

At last he heard footsteps crunching along the path. He peered carefully around the corner of the tombstone and quickly pulled his head back; the mysterious fat man stamped by so close to him that he could have touched him. The man again wore his cloak, and the cowl was pulled over his nose. From two holes in the hood his eyes glittered in the moonlight.

Flavius's friends also had noticed the fat man and were observing him from their hiding places. He made straight for the mausoleum and walked impatiently back and forth in front of it. Occasionally, he would stop a moment and listen. As if flung out of the earth, the Herculean ex-gladiator emerged from behind him and tapped him on the back. The fat man started and spun around.

"Hey, fatso, that lout Udo, Pollino's messenger, isn't coming," the boys heard the ex-gladiator say.

"Why not?"

"He must have eavesdropped on us last night. He's taken off. Friends of mine caught up with him and took him to Callon's."

"Why didn't you go and get Udo right away?" the fat man asked.

"You're a sly one, aren't you?" sneered the ex-gladiator. "Of course I tried to. I need my thousand gold pieces. I came too late; in the meantime, Callon had sold Udo to a couple of boys. But I took one of them by surprise in the Via Sacra and captured him. I've got him locked up, and I threatened to kill him if he didn't tell me where Udo was."

"Well, and so . . ." the fat man said.

"He's a hard nut, the punk. He's as silent as the graves here."

"I'll tell you what to do with him," the fat man said.

Caius's friends waited to hear what dreadful suggestion the fat man would come up with. As luck would have it, a metallic noise suddenly carried over to them from somewhere in the cemetery. Then it was still again. The fat man looked around nervously. "We'd better get inside there," he whispered to the ex-gladiator. They both disappeared in the mausoleum, and the boys couldn't hear them talking anymore. But the two reappeared in a short time and walked together along the center path where Mucius and Antonius were stationed.

Flavius breathed a sigh of relief. He was no coward; he had a part in all their adventures, but this time he shuddered at the thought of having to follow the fearsome ex-gladiator, a monster who threw a rope around one's neck or beat one to the ground with a single blow. To be on the safe side, he remained there a while longer; then he grabbed his stick and ran over to the mausoleum.

Publius, Julius, and Rufus were waiting there. In those last few minutes the moon had vanished behind a wall of clouds, and it had grown dark.

"I hope the gods stand by Mucius and Antonius," Flavius said anxiously.

"Don't worry," Publius replied. "They know well enough how dangerous these two characters are."

"On to Xantippus!" Julius said. He was second in command and led the boys when Mucius wasn't around.

"We're supposed to count to a hundred," Rufus reminded him.

"Oh, that's right," Julius said, and he began to count. But he got only as far as twenty. He was struck dumb and stiffened like a mummy in his tracks.

A form dressed in white rose from behind a gravestone and slowly turned its head, looking first this way, then that.

Only a Miracle Can Save Caius

"A ghost . . ." Flavius's gasp was almost soundless.

"Antonius seems to have been right," Publius whispered.

The ghost abruptly pulled a spade from under the white cloth that covered him. He bent over and started digging.

"By Pluto, that's no ghost," Rufus said. "It's one of those ghouls who rob graves."

"What vermin," Julius said. With all his might he hurled his big stick at the man like a spear. The blow sent the grave robber sprawling. He jumped up, threw his spade down, and fled in terror, leaping over graves and tombstones as he ran.

The boys bellowed with laughter.

"He thinks we're ghosts," Publius said mischievously.

"What a sly dog," Julius said. "He disguised himself as a ghost to scare off his brothers in the trade. These roughnecks really believe firmly in witches and ghosts." He went over and picked up his stick. "Let's go," he said. "Now to Xantippus!"

Xantippus was sitting on his bed and by the light of a flickering lamp was studying geometric figures on a roll of papyrus. He jumped up when his pupils burst into the room and came at them in a terrible temper.

"By all the Furies, where have you been so long?" he cried. "Why didn't you send me word immediately whether you'd got hold of Caius or not? I've been sitting here for five hours staring at my acute angles."

"We're sorry, Master Xanthos," Julius said. "But we've been to the cemetery on a mission of the greatest importance."

"Why? Did you want to get buried?"

"We were spying on the two conspirators," Publius confessed.

"Are you out of your minds, jeopardizing your lives like that? Where are Mucius and Antonius?"

"They're following the ex-gladiator," Rufus said.

"He's kidnapped Caius and taken him off somewhere," Julius said.

For the first time the boys saw Xantippus turn pale. "Taken Caius . . ." he said in distress. He sat down and ran trembling fingers through his gray hair. "That means you didn't get to him then."

Julius nodded. He explained what had happened. "Once we hear from Mucius and Antonius where the ex-gladiator lives, we'll free Caius by force," he concluded.

"That's madness," Xantippus said fiercely.

"Why?" Julius asked, shrinking away.

Xantippus explained what he meant. "First, the ex-gladiator has no house," he said. "He's as homeless as a stray dog, or he wouldn't find it so necessary to murder people for money. He probably rents a room somewhere, in a tenement or a cheap inn. Second, for this reason he wouldn't hold Caius prisoner at his place at all, but would take him to one of his rotten companions. Third, in consideration of your parents I absolutely forbid you to rush into any more dangerous situations. Your game of hide-and-go-seek at the cemetery was foolish enough."

Xantippus's sermon dashed the spirits of his pupils like a cold shower.

Rufus cried in despair, "But we can't sit around and wait until the gods save Caius by a miracle."

"Yes, you will, my son," Xantippus said. "You will do just that, sit around and wait. Now it's time for me to make a strong move. I personally will see to it that Caius is freed."

By Jupiter, Julius thought. *Does Xantippus be-*
lieve himself to be a god and able to work miracles?
Only a miracle can save Caius. Or does Xantippus
maybe want to challenge the ex-gladiator to a duel?

Xantippus continued. "One can best defang a
snake by stepping on its head. This murder is for
money merely. As soon as Mucius and Antonius
learn where the ex-gladiator lives, I'll go and offer
him two thousand pieces of gold to free Caius. I've
saved a little money, and it lies next door in my
secret chamber, where Udo is sleeping. Two thousand pieces of gold is twice the amount your mysterious fat man will pay the man to murder. An
assassination is far more complicated and dangerous
than what I will pay him for. He'll grab at the chance
with both hands."

"Senator Vinicius definitely will return your
money, Master Xanthos," Rufus said reassuringly.

"Under no circumstances would I accept it,"
Xantippus grumbled. "What's happened is partly
my fault," he added with a cough. "I should not
have allowed Caius to go to the prefect."

"With all due respect, Master Xanthos," Julius
said gravely, "but this time we, your pupils, must
not let you go."

"Am I hearing you correctly, Julius?" Xantippus
asked severely.

"The ex-gladiator will really grab you with both hands, but only to strangle you and steal your money. Then he'll go calmly ahead and kill Vinicius, too, and have three thousand gold pieces instead of two."

Xantippus gave a short laugh. "Julius, there's a saying that youths who have not yet grown a beard sometimes make the best philosophers. But you underestimate your teacher. I wouldn't think of taking the money with me. I'll tell the ex-gladiator that if he brings Caius the next morning to the great hall in the Julian Basilica and hands him over to me, he'll get his money. In the presence of judges, guards, and officials he'll think twice before trying to strangle me. But my plan is useless unless Mucius and Antonius come back," he added with concern.

"Let's hope the ex-gladiator hasn't taken them, too," Flavius said.

"They should have been here long ago," Publius said. "We left the cemetery at least a quarter of an hour later than they did."

He had scarcely spoken when they heard somebody speak behind the curtains: "Bravo, and that's as it should be." The next instant Antonius entered.

"The gods of the underworld cordially greet you," he shouted, laughing high-spiritedly, and he saluted with a sword like a victorious gladiator.

His friends were speechless.

Antonius was wearing breast armor and a helmet so big for him that it had slid down over his ears. He was holding a short double-edged sword in his right hand, and behind him, with his left, he was dragging a net weighted with lead balls. "Yes, take a good long look at me," he said, grinning, "for I've just had one foot in hell and escaped death only by a hair."

18

Memento Mori Is the Password

"Oh, you innocent lambs," Antonius groaned. "If only you knew what I've been through. It was crazy . . . just crazy!"

"What happened? Tell us. Tell us," his friends yelled.

Antonius burst out laughing. "I've come back from the jaws of hell," he said at last. "I should have been torn to shreds. But I've played a trick on them all." He laughed again and brandished the sword under Xantippus's nose.

Xantippus drew back. "Put that sword away," he shouted. "Where is Mucius?"

Antonius hurled the sword on the bed, tore off his helmet, and dropped onto an easy chair.

"Mucius took to the heels of the fat man. I followed the ex-gladiator," he panted.

"Did you learn where he lives?" Julius asked.

Antonius didn't reply. He stared a moment at

his friends. Then he said soberly, "Tell me the truth. Has my hair turned white?"

"Your hair is exactly what it's always been," Julius said consolingly.

"Just messier than usual," Publius added.

"That's because my hair was standing on end in fright," Antonius retorted. "My knees are still shaking, too."

"Pull yourself together," Xantippus said. "Where does the ex-gladiator live?"

"He lives in the amphitheater," Antonius said. "Way down below the arena in the catacombs."

"That's a blow," Xantippus said, greatly disturbed. "I can't get down there to speak to him. They wouldn't allow me in."

Antonious snorted. "You're right, Master Xanthos. It's worse than Hades. You might get in, all right, but you'd never get out. Caius is in the catacombs, too, locked in a cell."

"Oh, how hideous," Flavius cried.

"I tried to free him, but I'm afraid I failed," Antonius said sadly.

"How do you know he's jailed there?" Julius asked.

"Because I saw him."

"But how did you get into the catacombs?" said Publius. "Aren't they closely guarded at night?"

Antonius smiled. "I heard the ex-gladiator give the password. The password is Memento Mori. A perfect password. I stood eye to eye with a horrible death."

"Please tell everything calmly, Antonius, from the beginning," Xantippus said. "Why did Mucius go after the fat one, and you the ex-gladiator?"

"It was this way . . ." Antonius began explaining. He threw the net weighted with lead balls over a bust of Archimedes, which didn't exactly lift Xantippus's spirits, and then went on.

"We followed them closely to just in front of the Forum. They stopped in front of a tavern, and we hid behind a wine barrel to spy on them. 'If you don't find Udo and the letter before Pollino gets here, you're finished,' the fat man said. 'I'll find him soon enough, you can bet,' the ex-gladiator said. Then they separated. 'I must find out who the fat man is and where he lives,' Mucius whispered to me. 'He's one of the chief conspirators. You follow that other one.'

"He disappeared into the darkness, and I crept along after the ex-gladiator. Surprisingly, he stopped at the amphitheater and knocked on a side door. I quickly threw myself into a niche in the wall. 'The password!' somebody shouted behind the door. 'Memento Mori,' rasped the ex-gladiator. The guard let him in and closed the door. To be on the safe side, I stayed where I was a while longer, then I knocked, too. 'The password!' a voice sounded again. 'Memento Mori,' I replied hoarsely. The door opened, and I shot past the guard and ran down into a deep tunnel.

" 'Hey!' the guard shouted, but by then I'd already dashed around a corner into a long hallway. Not a soul was in sight in any direction. I heard only muffled roars and, from somewhere, laughter. On my right were doorways leading into rooms and on my left other doors fitted with peepholes and heavily bolted in front. I thought, 'Ah, those are cells for the prisoners. I bet the ex-gladiator has locked Caius in one of them. Maybe I can free him and we can escape together.' I crept from cell to cell, peering through the peepholes. In one I saw men lying on the floor moaning and crying. In another, people were on their knees mumbling prayers. I didn't see Caius among them, and I had to find him fast. I could hardly bear being in those catacombs any longer.

"Oh, friends, you can't imagine how grisly it was. The floor was slimy and it stank. The walls were damp, and water dripped on my head from the ceiling constantly. Scraps of food lay everywhere, and mounds of bones, looking like human skeletons. Fat rats stared at me evilly. I threw a bone at one to chase it away. It was dark, too, with only a few scattered flickering torches stuck in holders on the walls."

"You were very brave," Flavius said in admiration. "I'd have been afraid."

Antonius shook again with laughter. "That wasn't anything yet, my friend," he said. "You'd have dropped dead with horror. I almost did. But I gave it to them, those devils. Ha, ha, ha."

"You can tell us later about your heroic exploits," Xantippus said roughly. "Where did you finally discover Caius?"

"In one of the cells. He was lying on the hard stones and sleeping. I looked at the cell number: Number thirteen."

"Thirteen . . . an unlucky number," Rufus exclaimed.

"You're exactly right," said Antonius. "I was just about to shove back the bolt when in that instant I heard steps and saw two guards approaching on their rounds. I flew back to the tunnel I'd come from, but two gladiators appeared there.

" 'Oh, immortal gods,' I thought to myself. 'Now it's getting hot. Where can I hide?' I flattened myself against a door. The men hadn't seen me yet, but they were coming closer and from both directions. 'Oh, Jupiter, please turn me into a rat,' I pleaded. Unfortunately, I remained what I was, abandoned by the gods. That's how Odysseus must have felt between Scylla and Charybdis. In desperation I spun around, tore open the door behind me, stormed blindly into a room—and froze. I had stumbled into the gladiators' recreation room. I would have preferred leaping into the blazing crater of Vesuvius."

"Why? Did they do something to you?" Flavius asked anxiously.

Antonius laughed at him. "What do you think? That they kissed my feet? The whole bunch of them were drunk. Some, half naked, were rubbing themselves with oil, and others were drinking out of thick wineskins. Several were kneeling on the ground and tossing dice, and three or four close to a fire were turning half an oxen on a spit . . . It made me hungry to see it. Two were fighting; one had a short sword, the other just a net with lead balls in it. When they saw me, they all gaped as at a messenger from the underworld. Suddenly, a hand lifted me into the air by the collar, just as you'd grab a rabbit by the neck.

" 'Look what I've got,' he shouted. 'The kid is

a spy,' another sputtered. 'He's here to poison us so that we'll lose the fight tomorrow against the Spanish dogs.' The fellow who had hold of me started shaking me. 'Is that right?' he asked. 'I swear I've never even heard of Spanish dogs,' I protested, and they all guffawed at that. 'He swears . . . !' a giant bawled out, and leaped up on a table. He danced in a circle and snapped his fingers like a Spanish dancer.

" 'Search him,' a tall, thin man yelled, and the man who kept me dangling in the air reached his free hand into my coat pockets. 'No poison,' he yelled back in disappointment, 'only a piece of papyrus.' He dropped me and studied the papyrus. I held my breath. I had on Caius's cloak that Claudia had given me. 'What could Caius have written?' I asked myself. 'Certainly it must have been something innocent and stupid.' But I was very much mistaken. That piece of papyrus was my downfall."

Antonius paused and looked at his friends with a crafty smile. The boys were spellbound. Even Xantippus was impressed.

"Why was it your downfall?" Rufus asked.

"Everything in sequence," Antonius said. "On the papyrus were written the words: 'I, Caius, shall give no sassy answers in Xanthos's school.' " An-

tonius threw Xantippus a mischievous look from the corner of his eye.

"Ye gods," Xantippus said. "That was the sentence I gave as punishment for Caius to write last winter. He was to take the sentence home and copy it perfectly for me twenty times."

"I remember now, too," Publius chimed in. "He was angry about it on the way home from school and shoved the papyrus in his pocket rolled up into a little ball."

"He should have eaten it instead," Antonius went on. " 'Caius—he's that lout who dumped a jug of honey over our good friend Gorgon's head,' one of the gladiators snorted, bristling with rage. 'Gorgon locked him up in here someplace,' the thin one shouted. 'The punk was trying to escape. It's a good thing we caught him.' Several of these friendly fellows wanted to beat me black and blue. 'I've got a better idea,' the giant shouted, and he jumped down from the table. I think he was the ringleader of the bunch. 'Minimos!' he cried. And all at once a dwarf appeared from a room next door."

"A dwarf?" Flavius said in amazement.

"Dwarves are often matched in the arena for the amusement of the crowd," Xantippus interjected. "A disgusting spectacle. Go on, Antonius."

"The giant ordered the dwarf to go get a helmet

and breast armor. Before I'd even had time to protest wildly that I wasn't Caius, they stuck a gag in my mouth, tore off the sandals I'd wrapped around my waist, put the helmet on me, and clamped the armor on my chest. They stuck the short two-edged sword in my hand and hung the casting net with the lead balls over my head."

"Were you supposed to battle the dwarf?" Rufus asked.

"You've got another guess coming, my friend. That would have been child's play compared to what they had in store. Just wait. They dragged me out to the corridor, pushed open a thick wooden door, shoved me inside, and slammed the door. I stumbled down two stone steps, tangling myself in the net, and fell on my face. I lay there for a while and didn't move. I expected something bad. I heard a vicious, muffled growling. I sat up, but slowly. First I spat out my gag; then I looked around. It was almost dark; only two oil lamps were burning up near the ceiling. Again I heard growling, only this time more threatening, and cold chills ran along my back. I spotted caverns in the wall across from me, with iron bars in front of them. Suddenly, I knew where I was and my heart sank: the roughnecks had tossed me into a den of wild animals."

"Oh, no!" cried Flavius, his eyes big as saucers.

"Quiet, please," Rufus said hoarsely.

" 'They might want to just give me a good scare,' I thought. But that was wishful thinking. In some secret way an iron grille was raised in front of one of the caverns, and a lion sprang out with one leap. He sat down across from me and stared. I was paralyzed. All I could feel was the hair standing on end under the helmet."

Antonius paused and ran his hand over his hair, as though testing to see if it had since fallen into place again.

19

Everybody Cringes at the Sight of Antonius

Publius, Julius, Flavius, and Rufus waited to hear how Antonius saved himself. He must have escaped only by a miracle.

Outdoors, a column of farm carts rattled past. Then the warning call of a watchman resounded as it did at intervals all through the night: "Dear citizens of Rome," he droned. "Keep your fires banked and your lamps lit. Keep your doors and windows bolted so no evil may befall you."

Gradually, it grew quiet again. Behind the Viminal the sky turned rosy, the stars paled, and the first waking roosters crowed.

"Well, how did you manage to escape the lion?" Flavius asked.

"Through the grace of the gods and unbelievable luck," Antonius said.

"Come now," Publius said. "You aren't just handing us a pack of lies, are you?"

Antonius found this comment immensely funny. He doubled over with laughter. "You'll see soon enough that I'm not lying," he said. "Just hold your breath, you skeptic."

Baffled, Publius fell silent. What did Antonius mean by that?

"Why didn't you simply run out the door, Antonius?" Julius asked.

This question, too, evoked a great burst of hilarity from Antonius. "Have you ever sat across from a lion ready to pounce?" he asked.

"Thank Jupiter, no," Julius said.

"Then try it sometime," Antonius continued. "You wouldn't move a finger. Besides, the louts had barricaded the door from the outside. Even if they hadn't, before I could have turned around, I'd have been eaten alive."

"But how long can one sit motionless?" Rufus asked.

"I wondered about that, too," Antonius said. "All I knew was that the lion was not moving and had me fixed with his eyes. I stared back. I'd once heard that you should look an animal straight in the eye; then *they* get afraid. But I guess the lion hadn't heard that one. Apparently, the whole thing bored him, though, for soon he got up and loped over to the entrance of a tunnel along the left wall, where

he crawled inside—out of curiosity, it seemed. I
assumed it was a tunnel the big animals are driven
through on their way into the arena. Anyway, he
didn't get very far; an iron grille blocked his way.
He had forced himself so far into it, however, that
only his tail stuck out. I used this moment to make
a desperate attempt to save myself. I tore off the
net—here it is, you see—fled to the cavern the lion
had leaped from, and quickly climbed inside. I pulled
the sliding iron bars down again, and I was saved."

"Fabulous!" Julius, Flavius, and Rufus shouted.

"You did a beautiful job, Antonius," even Publius said.

Xantippus nodded his agreement. "Bravo, my
son," he added.

"What happened then?" Julius asked, greedy to
hear more.

"The lion came back and sat down in front of
his cage. Now it was I who was on the inside, and
he out. That must have confused him, for he looked
at me almost questioningly. 'Ha, so I've outwitted
you, you man-eater, eh?' I rejoiced to myself. I was
so happy that I stuck out my tongue at him. That
seemed to confuse the lion even more, but to me it
didn't matter. However, my high spirits didn't last
long. Suddenly, it occurred to me, 'By Pluto, now
I'm sitting safely in the cage, all right, but how am
I ever going to get out? Tomorrow they'll find me
and make hash out of me.' All at once the lion bent
his head to one side and gently rubbed against the
iron bars, as though asking me to be nice to him.
An insane ray of hope flooded through me. 'Can it
be?' I asked myself. 'No, it's impossible. Or is it
possible?'

"What were you thinking?" Flavius asked dumbly.

The others surmised some dark thing.

Antonius laughed again. "What was I thinking?
Nothing else. I merely looked at his paws; the claws

were snipped off and left completely blunt. 'Rameses!' I cried, almost crazy with joy.''

"Rameses . . . !" the others repeated, and they all began breathing regularly again as if a stone had been rolled away from in front of their hearts.

"Yes, that's who it was! It really was. He lay on his back and stretched all four paws in the air. He always did that when I used to play with him in the garden of the Numidian prince. 'Rameses,' I yelled, lifting up the bars and leaping down to his side. Overjoyed, I petted him, and he purred with pleasure. I think he was just as glad to see an old friend again as I was."

"Rameses? Is that the lion you wanted to give me as a birthday gift?" Xantippus asked.

"Yes, Master Xanthos. Apparently, my father had already sent him to the amphitheater."

"Antonius, you were really blessed," Rufus said with a beaming face.

Xantippus stroked his beard and smiled. "Here one can rightly say: 'He who is struck by lightning and not killed, he is holy.' Please continue, Antonius."

"Rameses climbed up on his hind legs and placed his huge paws on my shoulders, collapsing me like a straw. 'Poor Rameses,' I said, to comfort him. 'I'm sorry, but I must get away from here as quickly as

I can. I hope you understand. But I'll ask my father to come and get you.'

"I picked up the net, ran to the door, and jiggled it, but in vain. I'd forgotten it was bolted. Still, it had wide cracks in it. I lifted the sword, pushed it between the cracks—there where the bolt was—and succeeded in pushing it aside. Then I carefully opened the door and looked first to the right and then to the left. Nobody was in sight. I ran down the hall and then suddenly had an idea. 'If I'm fast, maybe I can free Caius,' I thought. Just then a door opened behind me with a crash, and I didn't even turn to see who it was but made for the tunnel that led to the exit door. Unfortunately, I had to pass the gladiators' room again. The door was open, and a beam of light cut across the hallway. Oh fates, that was a bad obstacle! I was going to steal by on tiptoe, and then it happened. My streak of luck reached its end, for two of the villains were standing in the doorway and saw me immediately. They gaped at me in astonishment. All at once they jumped back in horror and slammed the door with such force that plaster fell off the wall.

"'Aha,' I thought maliciously. 'They take me for my ghost returned from the underworld to take bloody revenge on them.' They couldn't believe I'd escaped the lion's den alive. I ran on, breathing

easier, dashed around a corner into the tunnel—
and collided with the two guards who were again
making their rounds. To my amazement, both turned
tail and skittered up a spiral staircase, three steps
at a time all the way, and vanished.

" 'Eureka! My ghost scared them, too,' I thought.
'I can understand that. I would run away, too, if I
met my ghost.' Now there was just one obstacle
remaining, and that was the sentinel at the door.
When I'd come in, though, I'd simply dashed past
him, and that seemed to have exasperated him. Then
I caught sight of him at the end of the tunnel sitting
on a stool near the door. Suddenly, I got a bold

idea. 'I'll sneak up to him, throw the net over his head, and shoot out the door. The net will make it hard for him to run after me.' I was just three steps away from the Cerberus when my helmet bumped against a wooden beam, poing!—I'd forgotten I still had it on—and the fellow shot into the air like a pitchforked elephant. 'That finishes me,' I thought. But miracle upon miracle, he saw me, tore open the door, and shot out into the Via Sacra faster than an arrow of Achilles. He leaped headfirst over a low wall and disappeared.

" 'What a coward!' I said to myself, and felt triumphant. 'No doubt he thought I was going to run him through with my sword. I'm a hero!' A little while later I was running across the Forum toward Broad Street. I'd just reached the speakers' platform, and a robber who must have been waiting for a victim to come by leaped out at me. 'Money or life!' he hissed like a dragon spitting fire. He threatened me with a club that was taller and fatter than I am. I raised my sword in fear, trying to protect my face, and abruptly the robber pulled away, threw down his club, and, tripping, crawled on all fours in a mad scramble to get under the platform. 'You miserable coward,' I bawled after him. 'Just come out here if you dare. I'll show you.' I was prouder than Mucius Scaevola after he'd slain the robber Cacus."

"I'm afraid I must remind you," Xantippus interrupted, "that it wasn't Mucius Scaevola but Hercules who killed the robber Cacus."

"It could be," Antonius continued. "At any rate, I was filled with pride. Still, I got away as fast as my legs would take me, just to make sure. And now here I am, ten times escaped from death."

Antonius beat himself on his breast armor like a victorious gladiator.

"Praise be Jupiter for smiling on you," Xantippus said.

"I'm sorry for the poor lion," Flavius said.

Antonius gave a wide grin. "What do you mean, the poor lion? He's sitting here right outside the door."

"What?" his friends shouted. They stared at the hanging, terrified.

Xantippus's eyes bulged. "What's the lion doing in front of my door?" he croaked.

"He's waiting for me," Antonius said. "He was running behind me like a dog the whole time without my even knowing it."

"Then the people weren't scared of you, but of the lion," Julius said.

"You guessed it," Antonius replied, snorting with laughter. "Nobody knew Rameses was tame. That's also what the crash was when I was running down the hallway away from the den—Rameses must have pushed open the door with his head in order to run after me. He was just as happy to get away from there as I was. May I let him in, Master Xanthos?"

"Eh . . . is it true he's harmless?"

"Not only harmless, but also well mannered. The only thing he can't stand is for somebody to lose his temper and yell at him."

Antonius jumped up, ran over to the door hanging, and pushed it aside. "Come here, Rameses. You may come in now."

At first an enormous lion's head filled the doorframe.

"Help!" Flavius squeaked, and he disappeared into Xantippus's clothes closet. Then Rameses appeared in his full majesty. He was a full-grown lion with a splendid dark brown mane.

Julius, Rufus, and Publius, frozen in their tracks, stared at him. Xantippus sat where he was with an iron stillness.

Antonius gave Rameses a pat on the head. "Please sit down," he said. "Hey, Publius, do you still believe I was handing you a pack of lies?"

Publius looked contrite.

Rameses sat down. Sitting, he came up to Antonius's forehead. "Thank you," Antonius said to Rameses, and threw himself back down on the easy chair. Rameses went over to him and lay at his feet. Antonius stroked him affectionately behind the ear.

Gradually Julius, Rufus, and Publius relaxed. They cautiously ventured closer to Rameses and at last stroked him.

"This is no lion, it's an overgrown lap dog," Publius said, grinning.

"Rameses saved my life," Antonius said. "I'll

never give him up again. Can he stay here tonight, Master Xanthos?"

"By Zeus and Apollo!" Xantippus moaned. "Are you out of your mind? Then I'll be sitting here not only with a slave around, but with a lion, too."

His students shouted with laughter.

"I can't take Rameses with me to Claudia's, Master Xanthos," Antonius pleaded. "She would be afraid; she's just a girl, after all."

"Claudia isn't afraid," Rufus interjected.

"All right then, Antonius," Xantippus said with a sigh. "Let him stay here for now, but don't forget to pick him up. Before you go to Claudia's, take him into my garden and tie him with the heavy wash line hanging out there. Make sure you attach the rope to the strongest olive tree you can find."

"Thank you, Master Xanthos," Antonius said happily. "Do you have anything for him to eat? He likes horsemeat."

"But I don't," Xantippus grumbled.

Publius, Julius, and Rufus laughed wildly.

"Quiet," Xantippus ordered them. "I do have a big leg of mutton you can give to Rameses later outdoors."

"Wonderful," Antonius shouted. "Roast mutton. That's his favorite dish."

Now Xantippus laughed, too. "Perhaps he'd like a jug of wine to go with his meal," he said.

Flavius poked his head out of the closet. His friends' gay laughter had charmed him out. But at the sight of the huge lion, he hesitated again. When Rufus sat astride Rameses' back and pulled him playfully by the ears, though, Flavius was sorry for having hidden at all. "I was only frightened because he's much bigger than I thought," he muttered.

The others politely didn't say anything; they themselves had been scared enough.

"Friends," Antonius shouted. "I'm jumping with joy already to think of what Mucius will say when he sees Rameses."

Xantippus, however, was troubled. "By all the gods, where can Mucius be?" he said.

The boys grew serious at once.

"I can't understand why he isn't here yet," Antonius said.

"I hope nothing's happened to him," Rufus added worriedly.

20

Riddle upon Riddle

After Mucius had separated from Antonius, he hurried along so as not to lose the fat man in the darkness.

The deserted Forum slumbered in the early glow of dawn. Even the multitude of colored marble statues all around seemed to be asleep.

The fat man was heading toward the massive building of the prefect.

Is it possible? Mucius thought. *Could he be the dreaded city prefect, Lucius Terrentius Manilius?*

His suspicion was confirmed in a surprising way. A rider on a white horse, covered with sweat, came galloping up to the fat man from the Via Sacra.

"Manilius! Manilius!" he shouted, still far off. "I bring an important message."

Manilius spun around. "What is it, Gaufrus?"

Mucius crouched behind a bench and peered around it. "By Jupiter, the mysterious fat man really is the prefect," he said to himself. "That's probably why he was so careful not to be recognized by the ex-gladiator."

As far as Mucius could make out, the horseman was an officer of the rural mounted police. He was covered with dust and exhausted; he must have been on the road for hours. He sprang off his horse and started talking excitedly to the prefect. Mucius was exasperated because he couldn't hear what the man was saying. The officer didn't remain long, but swung back into the saddle and galloped back the way he had come.

Manilius turned away from the prefecture, as though he had suddenly changed his mind, and rushed instead down Tuscan Street. Mucius followed. The pursuit led over the Velabrum, across the Forum Boarium, and ended behind Callon's slave shack on the Tiber, where the Egyptian bark was still bobbing at its mooring. Manilius stopped a moment and looked around intently. Mucius quickly hid in an archway. The prefect climbed over the railing of the bark and vanished into one of the cabins.

"What does this man have to do with the Egyptian bark?" Mucius wondered. Suddenly, it struck him that perhaps the ex-gladiator was holding Caius prisoner somewhere in the bowels of the ship. The cutthroat probably knew the sailors, and now Manilius wanted to cross-examine Caius himself.

"I must sneak on board and get to the bottom of it, no matter what," Mucius said. It was a bold undertaking, and so, using every precaution, he scrutinized the boat closely. Nobody was in sight but a lone sailor sleeping at the rudder. A dim band of light fell on the gangplank from the porthole of the cabin. The river washed against the boat with a gurgling sound. In the middle of the Tiber, almost parallel to the bark, rode the trireme at anchor, the Roman battleship with three tiers for the rows of oars manned by galley slaves. It was the patrol boat the boys had seen early in the morning rowing downriver.

"In an emergency I can swim over there," Mucius reflected. The Egyptian boat, smaller than the trireme, had only one tier of oars. From her forward deck rose a short mast. Approximately one arm's length below its tip hung a crow's nest. A huge box wrapped in canvas stood in front of the mast. "What could be in that box?" Mucius wondered. But he had more important things to do than concern himself with that. Nor did he wait any longer, but, stooping as he went, slipped hurriedly across the open space between Callon's shack and the boat, swung himself over the railing, and crawled like a snake on his stomach over to the cabin. He lay stretched out flat under the porthole so that the light wouldn't fall on him.

In the cabin two men were speaking. One was Manilius, the other an Egyptian. "Ammon," Mucius heard the prefect say, "we've got to leave. Pollino has been arrested."

"By Isis and Osiris!" the man called Ammon groaned. "Where did you learn that?"

"Gaufrus, a captain of the rural police who serves me faithfully, warned me in the nick of time just now. If Pollino betrays us, we're finished. If we leave immediately, we can still reach Alexandria before they catch up with us. Then we can disappear in Ethiopia as planned. The mighty arm of Rome doesn't reach that far."

"Absolutely, Lucius, my old friend, we'll set off at once. As captain, I'm responsible for my men," he replied. "But I still don't understand who would dare to arrest Pollino?"

"The senator Vinicius. It was at his command," Manilius explained. "Twelve cohorts of the Praetorian Guard took Pollino and his bodyguard prisoner at Veii, not far from the gates of Rome. Only Vinicius had the right to have General Pollino arrested. He is the proconsul and represents the Emperor. The Emperor is in Capri and gave Vinicius a completely free hand. Now I know, too, who the senator was whom Pollino wanted killed, and quickly: Vinicius, obviously. Somehow he must have gotten wind of Pollino's secret plan and told the Emperor."

"And now I, too, understand why they wanted to murder Vinicius," Mucius thought. "But what is the secret plan they're talking about?"

"Unluckily, that ex-gladiator Gorgon didn't find the messenger with the letter," Manilius continued.

Mucius inwardly rejoiced. "I guess we queered that one for you, eh?" he said to himself.

The prefect didn't say anything about Caius, though. The captain gave a command to somebody in Egyptian, a language Mucius couldn't understand. Instantly, a sailor shot out of the cabin, ran to the stern of the boat, and disappeared down a hatchway.

Nevertheless, Mucius was determined to remain where he was. He would have preferred leaving then, but he kept hoping to hear something about Caius.

"So we have to give up all our dreams of the riches Pollino promised us, Lucius?" Captain Ammon said.

"What good is all the gold in the world if you

pine your life away in a cell here in Rome?" Manilius replied with a grim laugh.

"What will become of Cerberus?" the captain asked. "It will be impossible to smuggle him into Egypt with us."

"There's no time to get him off our necks now," Manilius said. "We'll throw him overboard once we put out to sea."

"Cerberus . . . ?" Mucius wondered. "What, by Jupiter, is that supposed to mean? Riddle upon riddle." Mucius held his breath and listened. Manilius had mumbled something about Caius. Ammon said in reply, "And what's to happen to the boy Gorgon locked in the catacombs?"

Mucius was shocked. "Oh, how horrible," he thought. "Poor Caius! What catacombs could they have put him in?" He listened anxiously for Manilius's answer.

"I've given Gorgon the job of sending the boy into the arena tomorrow morning with all the other prisoners. Then we're rid of him for good. The boy knows more than is good for him, or for us."

"Oh, Jupiter," Mucius groaned. "Now I must get out of here. We must be there ahead of Gorgon. We must save Caius before tomorrow morning."

But it was too late. A dozen sailors had streamed

out of the hatch and spread over the deck like a swarm of frightened ants. At the same time, another group stormed over the pier onto the bark. Mucius's retreat was cut off. Nor did he dare slip over the other side to dive into the Tiber because it was teeming with sailors there, too. They would have caught him easily. Mucius pressed himself closer against the wall outside of the cabin and looked desperately for a hiding place. The sailors at the pier untied the line and shoved the boat offshore. Then they jumped on board, and the bark moved toward the middle of the river. An iron hammer struck an anvil with a resounding ring, in a body the oars shot out of the side hatches, and the ship headed downstream—first slowly, then picking up speed all the time.

"Fortune help me," Mucius whispered. "They'll catch me and lock me up in some hole. I'll be an unwilling passenger to Egypt. Or maybe they'll throw me overboard when we get out to sea—the mysterious Cerberus and me."

The oars slapped the water in rhythm to the hammer blows, and the houses along the harbor swept swiftly past Mucius's eyes.

All of a sudden a sailor leaned over him, grabbed him, and shouted something in Egyptian. Mucius tore himself loose and ran blindly to the foredeck. At first the sailor was confused, but then he ran after him. Other sailors joined the chase.

He heard Manilius thunder, "Seize him! Seize him! He's a spy."

Mucius bumped into the mast and caught sight of a rope ladder that led to the top. In his desperation he climbed up into the air with the speed of a monkey. At the top he forced himself through an opening in the floor of the crow's nest, got to his feet, and looked fearfully over the side. His heart sank to his knees; the sailors were climbing after him and already were reaching for the crow's nest with both hands. Mucius quickly unloosened the sandals still tied around his waist, pulled off his cloak, and at the moment that one of his pursuers rose through the floor of the crow's nest, he threw the heavy goatskin cloak over his head. He had won a reprieve. But the sailor shook himself wildly, and the cloak slid from his shoulders.

"I'm lost," Mucius said, shuddering. It was impossible for him to dive into the river from here— inevitably he would land on the deck and break every bone in his body. "Heavens, what can I do?" he stammered. The sailor jammed himself into the opening, and as the upper part of his body came into the crow's nest, he grinned triumphantly at

Mucius like a bloodthirsty pirate. Suddenly, the wooden underbeam of the Aemilius Bridge loomed up swiftly toward the ship, and in a flash Mucius saw salvation.

"I've got to try. It *must* work," he said, gathering courage. The bridge was already above him. He

ducked down, snapped himself up with a mighty bound into the air, clung to one of the crossbeams with his arms, pulled up his legs, and the bark hurtled away under him. The boat swept beneath the bridge and disappeared from his sight.

Mucius rejoiced. He was saved! He pulled himself up, crouched on a beam, and sighed with relief. "But how am I going to get out of here?" he wondered. He looked over at the crossbeams. Eureka! He could swing himself from one to the other all the way to the buttresses at the shore. Soon afterward his feet touched ground. Far in the distance he saw the mast of the Egyptian bark pull away behind the next bridge, the Cestius Bridge.

"May Neptune impale you on his trident on the way," he yelled after the boat, laughing scornfully. He was tired and felt as if he had been beaten. He sat down on a stone stairway leading to the river and rested.

The sun was just rising above the Palatine Hill, and the roofs and domes of the Imperial Palace glowed as though swept by fire. Hordes of slaves, armed with baskets and shopping bags, streamed across the Velabrum toward the marketplace. The fragrance of incense wafted toward Mucius from the Temple of Aesculapius on the Tiber island just opposite from where he was sitting. "The gods are being sacrificed to," Mucius reflected. "I should join the ceremony in gratitude." A violent fit of sneezing seized him, and that brought him back to his senses. He jumped to his feet and marched off, to get back to Xanthos's school as quickly as he could. But on the way he kept watching like an eagle to make sure the ex-gladiator didn't suddenly turn up and surprise him. Nevertheless, he hurried, for his friends were certainly waiting for him impatiently by now.

"Well, worrying won't harm them," Mucius muttered to himself as he trotted along Tuscan Street. "They've been lounging around the whole time while I nearly perished. Anyway, at least I've found out where Caius is." He couldn't know that Antonius had already beat him to it.

Nevertheless, Mucius had uncovered something of vital importance without at the moment being the least aware of what it was.

21

The Last Straw

Mucius's friends by now were more alarmed than ever over his being gone so long. They felt orphaned without him. Every once in a while, one of the boys would run out to Broad Street to see if he was in sight. Claudia, too, must have been at wit's end wondering why the boys were making her wait so long.

At least an hour had passed since Rufus and Antonius had taken Rameses out to the garden. The garden was surrounded by a wall, and people who went past outside couldn't see the lion. Antonius had tied Rameses to the thickest olive tree with Xantippus's laundry line, and Rufus had brought the leg of mutton from the kitchen. Rameses ate it in three seconds flat and, after finishing the meat, cracked the bone with his powerful teeth as though it were nothing but a bar of honeycomb. When the boys left him alone at last, he kept looking around for them expectantly. It seemed he couldn't believe that the paltry leg of mutton was all they had to offer him.

Grim-faced, Xantippus walked back and forth in his room. "By all the gods, where is Mucius?" he muttered darkly to himself.

Julius scratched behind his ear. "It's terrible for Caius to be held prisoner in the catacombs," he said. "Maybe for the time being we can't help him, but at least we know where he is. Only the gods know why Mucius isn't here yet."

"I know what happened to Mucius," Antonius cried excitedly.

"You do? Are you wiser than the gods then?" Publius said.

"The mysterious fat man isn't a man at all, but an evil spirit," Antonius went on, undeterred. "He noticed that Mucius was following him, so he had him turned into a snake."

"Why a snake?" Julius asked.

"A snake can't follow somebody very fast," Antonius explained. "No, I'm wrong. He turned him into a snail. That's even slower."

Flavius was impressed. "I hope he doesn't turn him into a statue," he said anxiously.

"A magician can't do that," Antonius said. "Only the gods can. If a magician did, the gods would punish him by chaining him to a rock and letting an eagle slash him to pieces as Zeus did to Prometheus for bringing fire to man."

"If you don't stop that drivel immediately, Antonius, I'll dish you out a juicy punishment," Xantippus snapped.

Antonius was crestfallen. Xantippus never appreciated the supernatural.

"Rufus," Xantippus said. "This time run to the corner of the Forum and look for Mucius. If you see him, race back here immediately and tell us."

"Yes, Master Xanthos," Rufus said. And he dashed out the door like an arrow.

Xantippus sat down and stared at the top of his desk in deep concentration. Outdoors, it was gradually becoming light. The sandals of early risers slapped against the pavement, and across the way the baker from whom the boys often bought rolls noisily flung open the shutters.

"We must free Caius from the catacombs as quickly as possible," said Xantippus suddenly.

"But how, Master Xanthos?" Julius asked. "Antonius told us it's crawling with murderous gladiators there. You must have overlooked that."

"Don't be impertinent, Julius," Xantippus said. "Antonius also told us those fellows were stupid drunk. It's still early. They'll be sleeping off their intoxication. That means we have one or two hours' time to attempt a rescue."

"We won't get past the guard at the door unnoticed," Publius interposed.

"I've been racking my brains over that one, too," Xantippus admitted. "If I hadn't, we'd already be on our way."

"I know what," Antonius said. "I just remembered something."

"So?" Xantippus said. "What do you know *this* time?"

"Udo told us he knows a secret route into the catacombs. He visited his father there secretly. His father was one of the animal keepers. If we were to find this secret route, we could outwit the guard at the door. Udo's way probably connects with the tunnel into the lion's den."

Xantippus nodded his agreement. "Very good, Antonius. You have a splendid memory. I've read somewhere before about this secret passageway into the catacombs. Allegedly, it is a canal through which water is released into the arena whenever a naval battle is staged. Regrettably, we don't know where the entrance to this canal is outside of the amphi-theater."

"We may not, but Udo does," Publius said, grinning.

Xantippus jumped to his feet. "Antonius! Fla-vius! Go quickly and get Udo out of the secret chamber."

"At your command, Master Xanthos," Antonius said. "But we have no idea where your secret chamber is."

"Run into the kitchen and roll the big cupboard to one side. The chamber is behind it."

Antonius and Flavius stormed into the kitchen.

Almost at once Antonius raced back into the

room. "Master Xanthos," Antonius cried. "The chamber is empty. Udo is gone!"

Xantippus fell back in his chair. "Gone? But great Jupiter, why?" he said.

"He must have fled through the garden and climbed over the wall," Julius said.

Xantippus murmured, "I would never have expected him simply to run away. Why would he leave?"

"I know. He stole your mathematical works in order to sell them and fled to Gaul with the money," Antonius offered.

Publius said, "He probably stole your two thousand gold pieces, too."

"That goes without saying," Xantippus said calmly, but he hurried into the kitchen with surprising agility for somebody his age.

When he returned, he looked considerably relieved. "Not the least thing is gone . . . except Udo," he said.

"I don't understand how Udo would dare let himself be seen on the street," Julius said. "He must know how risky that could be."

"If only he isn't working hand in glove with the conspirators," Publius said. "Perhaps Pollino smuggled him among us as a spy. His disappearance seems very suspicious to me."

"Don't talk such gibberish, Publius," Xantippus grumbled. "Pollino knows nothing at all about us. No, I assume Udo ran away because he's ashamed of being a burden on me. He has a good heart, that fellow."

Julius added, "In any case, it's no go with the passageway into the catacombs now."

"Caius is lost," Flavius muttered in defeat.

Xantippus pondered a moment and then said, "There's one last hope to cling to. And that is Caius's father. As proconsul, Senator Vinicius is the commander of the Praetorian Guard. If he sends two or three cohorts into the catacombs, even the gladiators would be powerless against them."

"But Vinicius is still in the Senate, and the session can last for days," Julius said.

"No, the session ends this morning," Xantippus said. "Today is the holy festival of the wine harvest. The Bacchanalia is a high feast day that even senators celebrate."

"Then maybe Vinicius is already home," Antonius exclaimed.

"It's even possible that Mucius is with Vinicius," Publius said. "He's forgotten that we're supposed to be here waiting for him and is waiting there just as anxiously as we are for him here."

"On to Vinicius," Flavius shouted, filling with hope.

The boys rushed to the door. "Wait," Xantippus thundered. "Put your cloaks on, and pull the hoods over your heads. I wouldn't like to hear of your running into the ex-gladiator's arms again."

That scared the boys, and they quickly put on their cloaks.

"Do you know what?" Antonius cried, suddenly inspired. "Why not take Rameses with us. He would scare even the fearsome ex-gladiator."

"Are you mad?" Xantippus said. "Today is a feast day. The streets around the Forum will be overflowing with people, among them many women and children. If you appear with the lion, there will be wholesale panic. Please, just leave Rameses in the garden."

Antonius was disappointed. "Then if I'm to bring him home, I won't be able to pick him up until tonight when it's dark," he mumbled.

"Go now," Xantippus said. "If Mucius comes, I'll send him to you. *If* he comes," he repeated with a sigh.

Footsteps sounded in the classroom.

"That must be Mucius," Flavius shouted ecstatically.

The hanging was flung aside, and the boys froze with terror. In the doorway stood the one-eyed ex-gladiator. Beside him was the dwarf Minimos. Each of them held a knife in his hand.

22

Thoroughness Sometimes Can Be Pushed Too Far

The boys stood rooted where they were, not daring to move a muscle. Xantippus had leaped to his feet in surprise.

Gorgon had planted himself in front of the classroom hanging like the monster Argus, except that Gorgon had only one eye to the hundred eyes of the beast.

"Where have you hidden the slave Udo?" he bawled. "Tell me or I'll cut off all your heads."

Minimos nodded with pleasure. "Pffft—one, two, three," he said. No bigger than a six-year-old, he had the voice of a veteran legionnaire.

"We don't know anything about a slave," Xantippus said scornfully. He gave a long look over at the bed where the two-edged sword lay that Antonius had thrown there. It was only an arm's length away from him.

"Don't lie to me, old Greek," Gorgon said. "My gladiator friends have shown me the piece of papyrus. The kid I nabbed is from your school. I also met Xanthos's pupils on the Forum with the slave Udo. Now answer me. Where is that tramp Udo?"

Antonius was preoccupied in thanking the gods that he had pulled the hood over his head, for otherwise the dwarf would have recognized him.

"I hope Gorgon hasn't discovered Caius is still locked up in cell thirteen," he thought.

Publius had noticed Xantippus eyeing the sword, and he came to his aid. Foolishly but courageously, he pretended he was going to leave in order to distract the ex-gladiator and the dwarf. He succeeded, but he paid dearly. They both rushed at him and beat him to the floor.

"You clown," Gorgon growled. "None of you is going to get away from me this time." He was about to give Publius another kick when Publius rolled nimbly out of the way.

Meantime, Xantippus had seized the sword and in a flash, his nostrils quivering, had gone after the intruders. "Now get out of here, you miserable gladiators," he thundered.

The sword was three times as long as the daggers, and it was a dangerous weapon. But the ex-gladiator was too agile for Xantippus. He grabbed

Flavius, who was standing closest to him, and put the dagger against his chest.

"Help!" Flavius squealed, turning white.

"Stay where you are and don't move, old man," Gorgon shouted at Xantippus, "or this boy has taken his last breath. Minimos, take away his sword."

The dwarf roughly tore the sword out of Xantippus's grasp and held it menacingly in his left hand.

Julius stole a look at the window. He was hoping a policeman would go by so he could call for help with all his lungs. But all he saw was Rufus. Rufus was looking cautiously over the edge of the window into the room. Suddenly he sped away like somebody chased by the Furies. "He's deserting us," Julius thought angrily, and it made him wonder. It was not like Rufus to leave his friends in a jam.

The ex-gladiator looked around with his one eye darting in a circle. "All right, make it fast!" he roared. "Will you tell me where Udo is or not?" He pointed the dagger at Flavius as if he were going to stab him. Flavius looked imploringly at his friends.

"Stop," Xantippus cried. "I'll give you two thousand pieces of gold if you leave us in peace and release the boy you have locked up in the catacombs."

At first Gorgon was taken off guard, but then he spat his contempt. "Your offer comes too late," he said. "That stubborn little punk is going into the arena this morning with the other prisoners who are sentenced to death."

How horrible, Antonius thought. *So the ex-glad-iator had noticed that Caius had not escaped.*

The boys stared at the ex-gladiator with hatred.

"You filthy hoodlum," Julius hissed, helpless in his rage.

The dwarf grimaced scornfully. "In the arena it's just like that—pffft, one, two, three," he said.

Xantippus was breathing heavily. "I'll make sure all of you are beheaded," he gasped.

"If you last that long," Gorgon said, giving a nasty laugh. "Your money would be as much use to me as a handful of ashes from hell. If I don't find Udo and the letter by the end of the day, I'll lose my own neck. I've committed myself to sending a famous senator into Hades."

His gaze happened to fall on the slate still hanging over the picture on the wall. "By Pluto and all the dogs of hell, everything I want to know is right over there!" he cried.

Now Xantippus cursed his habit of thorough-ness. He should not have written on the slate: "In Pollino's letter, brought by Udo the slave, the following names occur . . ." And farther down Caius, even more damagingly, had written with underlined letters:

"<u>V</u> i n i <u>c</u> i <u>u</u> s."

"Vinicius, ha!" Gorgon bellowed in triumph. "You shameless liar. So you do know Udo and you have read the letter. Vinicius! So that's the famous senator I'm supposed to murder. Now at last I can earn my thousand gold pieces. Hey, Minimos, we just walked past the Senate. The gates will be opened soon, won't they?"

"Just like that—pffft, one, two, three," the dwarf said. "Hurry, Vinicius will be coming out soon."

Xantippus and the boys were shattered. All their efforts to save Caius's father had failed. And Caius himself was hopelessly lost. Perhaps at least they could still warn Vinicius in time if only the ex-gladiator wasn't here. But Gorgon was thwarting them in that, too.

"Minimos," he rasped. "You hold the boys here, and use your dagger if one dares to say a word. Wait here for me until I get back . . ." He broke off with a start.

Someone struck his shoulder through the hanging with such force that he stumbled forward. He turned and shrieked, "You miserable dog! Whoever you are, I'll strangle you."

He yanked the hanging to one side and bounded backward with a scream. Sitting in front of him, crouching to attack, was a powerful lion with its tail whipping furiously from side to side. Behind the lion stood Rufus with a long piece of wash line bunched in his hand. Before the ex-gladiator could flee, Rameses leaped straight at him through the air. Gorgon tipped backward and fell. Rameses lay on top of him and snarled at him with open jaws.

"Help!" the ex-gladiator gurgled. His eye was bulging in terror. "Minimos, help!" he rattled in his throat. But the dwarf had long since vanished. He

had dropped dagger and sword, hurtled out the window with one leap, and fled.

The boys danced around the room in jubilation.

"Praised be Rameses, the jolly good lion," Julius shouted.

"And praised be Rufus," Flavius moaned. His whole body still was trembling.

"Rameses, you gave a great performance," Antonius said.

Xantippus was pretty anxious, though. "Are you sure he won't take a bite out of him?" he asked.

"Of course he won't," Antonius said, beaming with pride. "He learned what he's doing from a lion tamer. He's angry only because the brute shouted at him. You can stick your head into Rameses' jaws without a worry."

"Thank you," Xantippus said. "I'll forgo the pleasure. Pull the lion off the man before he smothers."

"It would serve him right," Flavius and Rufus chimed in together.

"Quiet now," Xantippus said. "We'll tie and gag this thug and lock him in the secret chamber. Vinicius will have him picked up by the Praetorian Guard."

"Help me, help me! Have mercy on me," the ex-gladiator begged with the last of his strength.

Rameses' hot breath was blowing in his face, and his strong white teeth hovered over Gorgon only a menacing nose's length away.

Antonius thumped Rameses on the back energetically. "Behave yourself, Rameses," he exhorted, and tugged at the lion's mane.

Julius, Publius, and Rufus joined forces and pulled Rameses by the tail. Rameses got off the ex-gladiator reluctantly, but he lay down as close as he could get and stared at him attentively.

Gorgon stood up groaning.

Xantippus quickly recovered the sword. "One movement from you and I'll stab you," he warned.

Publius and Julius armed themselves with two daggers.

"Let me live! Have pity on me!" Gorgon pleaded.

"You had no pity for Caius," Flavius yelled.

"He dumped a jug of honey over my head." Gorgon groaned.

"He should have dumped something else over your head," Publius hissed.

"Cut the wash line in half," Xantippus said. "You'll need the one half to tie the lion up outside again."

Julius cut the wash line in two, and Rufus and Antonius wound one half around the ex-gladiator at least twenty times so he ended up looking like the

Laocoön entangled by the serpents. As a final measure, they pushed a gag in his mouth. Then all together they dragged him across the floor into the kitchen, packed him away in the secret chamber, and pushed the cupboard in front of the door.

"So, now we've turned the tables," Publius said, rubbing his hands in glee.

"At any rate, we've stopped them from killing Vinicius," Rufus said.

"Getting Rameses was a fabulous idea, Rufus," Julius said.

Rufus beamed. "I saw the terrible straits you were in through the window," he explained. "At first I started running around looking for the police. Naturally, there were none to be found anywhere. Then I ran through the little gate into the garden and let Rameses loose."

"Why didn't you come in with him through the kitchen?" Julius asked.

"I had seen the ex-gladiator was standing in front of the hanging to the classroom," Rufus said. "From there, he could have seen me in time and threatened to stab Flavius if I dared to come closer with the lion. That's why I took Rameses with me down the street and slipped in through the classroom."

Rufus grinned in delight. "I'll tell you, the people in the street scattered, though, when I appeared with the lion. Fortunately, there were no children around. Two men clambered into a house through the window. Another crawled into an empty wine barrel. A woman collided with our baker just as he was carrying out a plate of freshly baked little cakes. They bounced against each other and fell, together with the cakes."

The boys doubled over with laughter. It was a reaction from the fear they had gone through.

Xantippus yelled into the kitchen, "Stop all that chatter. Caius is in grave danger. Have you forgotten?"

Stricken, the boys quieted at once. Antonius took Rameses and the other half of the wash line, and the boys tied him again to the olive tree.

"Julius, you still have the rest of our money," Antonius said. "We have to give Rameses something to eat."

"He's really earned it," Flavius exclaimed.

They ran down Broad Street to the closest butcher and bought him a mountain of bones and trimmings for the ten sesterces.

Rameses plunged into the food greedily.

"Now he'll be satisfied for a while," Antonius said.

When they returned to Xantippus, Mucius was talking excitedly to him.

"Mucius!" the boys, in delirious unison, cried. They would have liked to lift him on their shoulders and carry him around in a circle.

"Well, at last you're back again," Julius said. "We've certainly been worried about you."

"I almost landed in Egypt," Mucius said seriously. He had just told Xantippus about his adventure on the ship and what he had learned about Caius's fate.

Xantippus sat gloomily and stared in front of him, lost in thought.

"Riches . . . riches . . ." he muttered over and over. "Something's dawning on me."

The boy didn't notice. They had Mucius again, and for them that was the main thing.

"Where have you been so long?" Julius asked.

"And why would you have landed in Egypt?" Antonius cried excitedly.

"Tell us! Tell us!" Flavius and Rufus shouted.

"We don't have time," Mucius said. "I'm afraid we have to get to Claudia's immediately. It's no use. We have to bring her the bad news of what's happened to her brother."

"That won't be necessary," someone said.

The boys spun around, flabbergasted.

Standing in the doorway was Caius, pale and haggard, but unharmed.

23

A Distressing Turn of Events

The boys could not believe their eyes. How could Caius still be alive? A miracle of the gods must have occurred.

"It's not really him, it's his ghost," Antonius mumbled.

But Xantippus was not about to believe in ghosts. Beaming, he cried, "By the golden light of Helios! What a wonderful surprise to have you back, Caius! We'd despaired of ever seeing you again."

"Udo saved me."

"Udo?" His friends were dumbfounded anew.

"Then it was because of you that he disappeared from here," Julius asked.

Caius nodded.

"How did he know you were locked up in the catacombs?" Publius asked.

Caius lowered himself to the bed and gloomily stared at the floor. Inexplicably, he seemed unhappy about his rescue. He began speaking. "Udo listened through the wall next door in the secret chamber and heard Antonius say I was in cell thirteen. With that, he took right off. About an hour ago he quietly opened the door to my cell and motioned for me to follow him.

"The gladiators were all still sleeping. Udo knew when the guards made their rounds past my cell. Then he brought me back into the open air through an underground canal."

"The secret passageway . . . !" Antonius cried.

"But where is Udo?" Xantippus asked with concern. "Why didn't he come with you?"

"He went back into the catacombs again. He didn't say why."

"He must be mad to risk his life a second time," Antonius said.

"I came through a manhole into daylight in a lonely little street in Subura," Caius resumed. "I ran home as fast as I could. I was afraid the ex-gladiator might still be after me."

"You're in for a surprise now, Caius," Julius piped up. "We've put an end for all time to that cutthroat's handiwork."

He gave Caius a quick account of the terrifying visit the ex-gladiator and Minimos had paid on Xanthos's school and of Rameses' triumph.

"Just think," Antonius exclaimed, laughing. "The ex-gladiator wanted to cut off our heads."

"Go ahead and laugh," Flavius broke in angrily. "I'm the one he almost stabbed."

Caius was half listening. Hunched over the bed, he sat and stared before him, looking depressed.

"So? You've taken him prisoner," he muttered. "Of course I couldn't have known that. That's why, as a precaution, I had four of our slaves bring me to you in a closed sedan chair."

"Claudia must have been ecstatic to see you," Rufus said.

Caius didn't answer. All he did was sigh deeply.

His friends were puzzled. They thought Caius still was suffering from his experiences in the catacombs. He was a tough, brave young Roman, to be sure, but one night in the catacombs could make even a grown man fainthearted.

"I've got a great idea!" Antonius burst out, casting a sidelong glance at Caius. "Today we'll throw a terrific feast, either at my house or at Mucius's. We'll make a celebration fire in the garden and dance around it."

"And before we eat, we'll offer the gods our thanks," Flavius said.

"We've got every reason in the world to celebrate," Julius cried enthusiastically. "Caius is saved, Mucius is back with us, the thug Gorgon is locked up, and your father, Caius, is no longer in danger."

"From now on all is nectar and ambrosia," Antonius said, rejoicing.

"We should invite Claudia to the feast, too," Rufus said.

"And Master Xanthos," Mucius said. "Without him we would have been helpless."

"Thank you," Xantippus said. "But I don't like to dance, and certainly not around a fire."

The boys laughed loudly—all except Caius. Then all at once he began to cry. His friends were aghast.

"What's the matter?" Flavius asked anxiously.

"Dear friends," Caius said between sobs, "I've come back only to bid you all farewell forever." He tried frantically to control his sobs.

"What . . . what do you mean?" Mucius stammered.

"My father, Claudia, and I are all lost," Caius said in a monotone. "A grim fate awaits us."

Uncomprehending and troubled, the boys stared at him.

Xantippus was deeply disturbed. "Pull yourself together, Caius," he said gently. "What has happened? Why are you lost?"

"My father can't find the treasure of a hundred thousand gold pieces Governor Pollino embezzled."

"Ah, so those are the *riches* Captain Ammon was talking about," Xantippus said. "Now I understand. This all concerns the gold that disappeared eleven years ago in the battle in the Teutoburg Forest. Is that it, Caius?"

"Yes," said Caius. "Ten legionnaires had buried the gold so it wouldn't fall into the hands of the Germans. Of those ten only one is alive—the prefect Manilius. He waited until his brother-in-law Pollino was made governor. Then he told him about the treasure and agreed to share it with him."

"Where have you suddenly learned that?" Julius asked in astonishment.

"Tiro told me a while ago. My father trusts him completely."

"But your father had Pollino arrested in Veii," Mucius said. "Why doesn't he make him tell where the money is?"

"Pollino is dead," Caius said.

"Dead?" the others repeated.

"He fell on his sword right after he was taken prisoner," Caius resumed in a faltering voice. "Once he had dug up the gold, he told no one where it was hidden, not even Manilius. My father learned some time ago from one of his spies that Pollino had discovered the ten million sesterces, and so my father told the Emperor. The gold belongs to the Emperor, and he needs it badly. All this had to remain a state secret as long as Pollino was free. He couldn't be arrested in his fortress in Germania; it's protected by ten regiments of his legionnaires. The Emperor and my father had to wait until he came to Rome."

"He was going to escape to Ethiopia with Manilius," Mucius said.

"My father didn't know that," said Caius.

"But how can you say you're lost and are awaiting a grim fate?" Julius asked.

"The Emperor has demanded that the gold be found by the time he returns from Capri, and he arrives tonight."

"It's not your father's fault that he can't find the gold," Mucius said.

"You don't know the Emperor," Caius said softly.

"Oh yes I do," Julius muttered, looking anxiously around.

"Just as I got home, my father was coming back from the Senate," Caius continued.

"Did your father know he was marked for murder?" Julius interrupted.

"No," Caius said. "He was shocked when I told him. 'By Pluto!' he cried. 'Pollino's spies have been working, too. But at last we have him in our power!' My father had hardly spoken when the centurion Marcus Turnus appeared—he was the commanding officer of the Praetorians who, on my father's orders, captured Pollino at Veii. He told him of Pollino's suicide. My father turned as pale as this bed sheet.

'Now I'll never find the gold!' he said. 'I'm lost! Caius and Claudia and I will be sent by the Emperor into the marble quarries at Paros, sentenced to a life of hard labor.' "

"Horrible!" Flavius groaned.

"What a shocking turn of events," Xantippus said huskily.

"Claudia couldn't survive the strain for fourteen days," Rufus stammered.

"Then we must save her and Caius, too," Mucius said resolutely. "This instant, before it's too late."

Antonius proposed a plan of action. "We can hide you in our cave today. Once night comes, disguised as beggars, you'll flee into the hills. Claudia must cut her hair and dress like a boy. We'll take a scissors along."

"Claudia will have her own scissors," Publius said.

Antonius replied irritably, "They might be dull."

"And you are dull-witted," Publius retorted.

"Quit arguing over stupid scissors," Mucius barked at them. "We must get going at once. Come on, Caius."

"No, thank you. You're troubling yourselves for nothing. I'm not going to leave my father alone. I've got to help him in the marble quarries. My father is sixty. Claudia, too, has sworn that she will never abandon him. My father told us to run away, but for the first time we've disobeyed him."

"We'll save your father, too," Rufus shouted. "We'll hide all three of you."

"Will you?" Caius said, looking up hopefully.

"What an idiot I am," Mucius put in. "I should have thought of that immediately. Of course, we'll save all three of you."

Julius protested, "But we can't take them into our cave. It's too close to Vinicius's villa. The Emperor's police dogs will sniff around the whole area."

"I've got a better idea," Antonius said. "We'll hide them over there in the house of the dead magician, Lukos." He pointed out the window to a towerlike building diagonally across from Xanthos's school. "It's been deserted since Lukos's death. Nobody ever goes in there. Everybody knows it's haunted by Lukos's ghost, and the ghost of a magician is especially terrifying."

"We don't have time to worry about ghosts now," Mucius said. "There is nothing worse than the marble quarries at Paros. Lukos's house will make a perfect hiding place."

Mucius broke off and shot Xantippus a questioning look. The others were anxious to know, too, what their teacher thought about their plan.

To their astonishment, Xantippus was scribbling mysterious numbers on a piece of papyrus. He was so absorbed in what he was doing that apparently he had not been listening to the boys at all. His pupils were surprised at him—could he have lost interest suddenly in the fate threatening Vinicius, Caius, and Claudia?

But they were very much mistaken. Xantippus was making a desperate attempt to find a happier solution to the problem of the Vinicius family.

24

How Much Does a Bear Weigh?

Claudia was kneeling in front of the family altar when the boys stormed in.

Since Xantippus had seemed loath to even hint to them what suddenly possessed him, they had left him mulling over his mysterious figures. They had gone to get Vinicius and Claudia and guide them to Lukos's house.

At the Forum they were caught in an enormous crowd and nearly crushed to death. The Bacchanalia was in full swing. Swarms of citizens—men and women, many with garlands of vine leaves on their heads—pushed and crowded around the vendors' booths. The merchants were shouting themselves hoarse in praise of their wares.

The smells of grilled meat and sausages, onions, fresh rolls, and roasted chestnuts filled the air. Clowns, grotesquely made up and wearing pointed hats, reeled around on stilts, bawling out bawdy songs. Many children sat on ponies decorated with colored feathers, and they recklessly forced themselves through the crowds. Everywhere dogs leaped and yelped. On the speaker's platform at the foot of the Temple of Jupiter was a band. Trumpets blared, flutes trilled, and bronze cymbals banged together with a crash. The noise was so deafening that Flavius had to plug his ears with his hands. The one sour note in the whole celebration was a black thundercloud that rose threateningly behind the Janiculan Hill. Now and then streaks of lightning darted fiercely across the sky.

"All these people have gone mad," Rufus roared, in order to make himself heard. He was furious because everybody was having a good time while he and his friends from Xanthos's school were fearful for the lives of their friends, Caius and Claudia.

Mucius, though, was delighted. "This maelstrom of people is made to order for us," he said. "Vinicius, Claudia, and Caius can easily be lost in this crowd. But they must put garlands on their heads, too."

The guard at the door of the Villa Vinicius let them in this time without a word. He just stared at them absently. The other slaves, too, looked at them with haggard faces. Their future was gloomy indeed if their master was to be exiled.

Once in the main hall, the boys waited for Claudia to finish her devotions. Lysis stood beside her with her head bowed. They were alone.

"Claudia!" Antonius cried as they got to their feet at last. "Quickly, you must cut your hair. From here on you're going to be a boy."

Claudia spun around. Her eyes were wet with tears, and she looked pale and careworn. She wore a plain dark-colored tunic and slippers. The artfully piled curls of yesterday now were pathetically disarranged.

"Why must I be a boy?" she asked wearily.

"We're running away immediately," Caius said. "Where's father? He must come with us."

Claudia sat down. She threw her hands over her face and sobbed bitterly. "You've come too late," she finally managed to say. Then, overcome with grief, she could not go on.

"Why is it too late?" Caius asked, suddenly panicky.

"Young master," Lysis said, "Tribune Lucius Octavius Veranus is here, accompanied by two higher officers."

"What do they want?" Caius asked, but he knew only too well what they wanted.

"The Emperor has arrived sooner than expected.

He's been in Rome since this morning and has sent the tribune and the officers to arrest our master, you, and Claudia," Lysis answered.

Caius turned pale. His friends were at a loss for words. Thunder rumbled far off in the distance.

All at once a louder thunder sounded behind the hanging in front of the vestibule.

"Let me through, you pig-headed nincompoop," somebody bellowed. And Xantippus tore into the room like a god bent on revenge.

"Master Xanthos," Claudia exclaimed incredulously.

"Xantippus!" the boys all stammered.

"Where's your father, Claudia?" Xantippus panted. He was absolutely winded. He had run all the way like a marathon runner.

"My father is being arrested by a tribune and two officers," Caius said.

"Nonsense and idiocy," Xantippus said. "Get your father in here at once. I know where the gold is."

Claudia sprang up. "You know where the gold is?" she repeated, her voice quivering.

"Don't ask questions. Go get your father," Xantippus thundered.

Claudia skimmed across the hall to the door of

her father's room. "Father!" she cried. "Father, come out at once. Master Xanthos is here, and he knows where the gold is."

The door was flung open, and Senator Vinicius appeared. A big man, he was somewhat on the heavy side. His hair was white and his eyebrows black, features that had always greatly impressed the boys. Now he was pale but composed. He walked quickly to Xantippus. The tribune, Lucius Octavius Veranus, and the two officers followed, all armed with long swords. Tiro emerged behind them with the centurion Turnus, commanding officer of the Praetorian Guard.

"Did I hear correctly, Master Xanthos?" Vinicius asked. "You know where the gold is?"

"I figured it out just ten minutes ago," Xantippus replied, still breathing hard.

"Please sit down, Master Xanthos." The senator pushed up a chair for him. He was an educated man and treated the famous mathematician Xanthos, his son's teacher, with great respect.

Xantippus sat down. He panted, then continued with his explanation.

"Ever since Udo, when first telling us about Pollino, mentioned the bear and the cage, I've gone on turning that story over in my mind."

"You are speaking of the brave slave who rescued my son from the catacombs, Master Xanthos?"

"I'm speaking of the bear and the cage," Xantippus grumbled.

"This is the first I've heard about a bear in a cage," Vinicius said. "What about it?"

"No more than that the hundred thousand gold pieces are hidden in the cage."

"What?" Vinicius said. "How do you know?"

"The cage has a double floor, and the ten million sesterces can be found in the space between. The reason the bear is there is so that nobody will enter the cage."

Vinicius's eyes widened. "How did you arrive at the notion that the gold is in the cage?" he asked, still reluctant to believe in miracles.

"I just told you, I figured it out. I posed a few questions and juggled around some figures. Udo was in Germania when twenty-four legionnaires lifted the cage with the bear in it onto a wagon. There were twelve oxen harnessed to the wagon."

"I said at the time that it wasn't a bear but a mammoth," Antonius piped up.

"Quiet," Xantippus said. "I forbid any more interruptions. Question number one I asked myself was as follows: How much does a bear weigh? Answer: A fully grown brown bear weighs no more than four hundred pounds. Question number two: What does a cage weigh? Answer: It weighs two hundred pounds at most. Good. All together that makes six hundred pounds. Question three: How many legionnaires would it take to lift approximately six hundred pounds onto a wagon? Answer: Six. Any legionnaire worth the name is capable of lifting a hundred pounds. Question number four: How many oxen are needed to pull a wagon with a load of six hundred pounds? Exactly four. Question number five: Why, then, by Pluto, Poseidon, and the Furies, must twenty-four legionnaires lift the bear and the cage onto the wagon? There was only one explanation: the bear and the cage weigh not six hundred, but three thousand one hundred pounds."

Vinicius and the others listened with growing astonishment.

Nevertheless, Vinicius was confused and took the liberty of interrupting Xantippus. "Three thousand one hundred pounds, you say, Master Xanthos? How do you explain this disparity in weight?"

"I'm coming to that," Xantippus grumbled. "Now, here at last we come to my figures. A: One gold piece weighs a fortieth part of a pound. B: Therefore, one hundred thousand pieces of gold weigh . . ."

"Two thousand five hundred!" Vinicius shouted, thunderstruck.

"Excellent, Senator. You are a marvelous calculator," said Xantippus appreciatively. "Therefore, including the cage and the bear, that makes three thousand one hundred pounds. According to the laws of logic and mathematical proofs, this then is the indisputable fact: Pollino hid the gold in the cage and had it carted away."

"Jupiter!" Vinicius exclaimed. "Master Xanthos, I am at a loss for words to thank you."

Claudia, who had scarcely dared breathe because of the tension, rushed over to Vinicius. "Oh,

Father, Father." She sobbed. "Master Xanthos has saved our lives." She was crying again, but this time with joy.

Caius smiled with happiness and relief from ear to ear.

Lucius Octavius Veranus was delighted, too. As a close friend of Vinicius, he had obeyed with heavy heart the Emperor's order to arrest the senator, Claudia, and Caius.

"At last now I, too, understand what Pollino meant," said Centurion Turnus. "When Pollino was lying on the ground, I leaned over him and said, 'Confess where the gold is, you traitor!' 'It's behind bars,' he said—his last words, the death rattle already in his throat. Now I know he meant the bars on the cage."

Vinicius had suddenly become doubtful. "But where is the cage, Master Xanthos?"

"Udo told us that, too," Xantippus replied, pulling on his beard with satisfaction. "The cage with the bear in it is in the zoological garden here in Rome, in the park of Sallust. Why Pollino had the gold taken there, I don't know. All I know is that the bear is guarding it like the hound of hell, Cerberus."

"Stop!" Mucius shouted wildly.

Everyone was brought up short.

Only Xantippus was not. "See here, Mucius," he said. "What do you mean by this outburst? What utter lack of discipline!"

"Forgive me, Master Xanthos," Mucius sputtered. "The cage with the bear is not in the zoological garden."

25

Caius Sees Another Light

"The cage is not . . . in the zoological gardens?"
Xantippus stuttered in disbelief.

Vinicius was alarmed. Claudia grew pale again
and clasped her father's hand. Caius stared at Mucius with his mouth hanging open.

"But, Mucius, you yourself heard Udo say Pollino sent the cage to the zoological gardens," Xantippus said.

"It never got there," Mucius continued. "But I
know where it is."

Claudia, near despair, cried out, "Mucius,
please . . . please . . . where, oh, where is it?"

Mucius said, "It's on the Egyptian bark. Now I
understand everything. When Master Xanthos was
talking about Cerberus, the dog of hell, Captain
Ammon's question to the prefect came back to me:
'What will become of Cerberus?' Also, I remember
the big strange box lying under the canvas on the

deck. That could only have been a cage. Pollino's intention was to flee to Ethiopia without Manilius and Ammon guessing what was inside. Ye gods, but I'm glad I sneaked onto that bark."

"Where is the bark?" Tribune Veranus asked.

"It's just now going down the Tiber toward the harbor at Ostia," Mucius said.

"Veranus," Vinicius said, his eyes shining with determination, "a trireme from the war fleet is docked at the harbor near the Forum Boarium. It's one of the fastest patrol boats we've got. We can easily catch the bark before it reaches Ostia."

"On with it then," the tribune shouted. "We'll take Manilius and Ammon prisoner and have the cage with the money taken to the Emperor's palace."

Vinicius, Veranus, the two officers, and Turnus hurried to the door.

"Father," Claudia cried, "what will happen to the poor bear?"

Vinicius turned with a laugh and called back, "Don't worry, Claudia. I'll see to it that he lands in the zoological garden where he belongs." Then he disappeared with the others.

"Oh, what a mess," Julius said, looking confused again. "Now what are we going to do with Gorgon, Master Xanthos? He's still in your secret room, tied and gagged."

"That's right," Xantippus said, and he scratched behind his ear.

"That will be taken care of, too, Master Xanthos," Tiro said. "When my master returns, he'll order a cohort of the Praetorian Guard to take that murderer to Mamertine Prison. They'll jail him there in an isolation cell deep in the darkest cellar, and he'll go before a judge next week."

"Perfect," Xantippus said. "I'll be home in half an hour at the latest and show them the secret room then."

"Please be careful that the Praetorians don't do anything to Rameses," Antonius said.

"I imagine they will be glad if he doesn't do anything to them," Xantippus said.

Claudia was quite moved. "Master Xanthos," she said, "I'll never forget what all of you have done for us."

"You can thank my pupils," Xantippus said with a smile. "If they hadn't bought me Udo for a birthday present, we would never have found out where the gold is."

The boys gathered around him.

"Master Xanthos," Mucius said, "that was certainly a surprise when you suddenly burst in here like a god coming to the rescue. We thought you had lost all interest."

"You should certainly know me better than that. By the way, I have another surprise for you. Udo is sitting outside."

"Udo!" the boys all shouted in delight.

"He came in five minutes after you ran off," Xantippus said.

"Why did he go back into the catacombs?" Caius said.

"He still had to free the other prisoners."

"By Hercules," Julius said, panicking again. "Udo! So here we are again sitting around and not knowing what to do with him."

"That's no problem at all," Xantippus said. "I'll buy him from you. What do you want for him?"

"Five hundred sesterces," Julius said quickly.

Xantippus frowned. "What? I thought you only paid four hundred and fifty for him."

"Prices have gone up since yesterday," Julius replied, looking innocent.

Xantippus said, "No deal. Unfortunately, *my* prices have gone up in the meantime, too."

"Your prices? What prices do you mean?" Julius said.

"Give me a wax tablet and a stylus."

Tiro hurried to the next room and brought back the writing material.

Xantippus again began scribbling a column of figures. "My price is exactly right," he said, and added, "That is to say, you owe me money." With a flicker of a smile crossing his face, he read aloud: "A: I put out a hundred and twenty sesterces for a jug of honey; B: seven sesterces for a new chair because Caius knocked over the old one and broke it; C: thirty-five sesterces for a new bed sheet— Antonius threw the sword on the bed and ripped it; D: food and lodgings for a hungry young slave—for decency's sake I'm charging you only fifty sesterces for that."

The faces of the boys were growing longer than Xantippus's bill.

"E: two hundred and fifty sesterces for my best olive tree which Rameses completely ruined by scratching on it, and at that you're getting away cheap."

"But Rameses' claws are trimmed." Antonius interrupted him indignantly.

"That's just it. He kept scratching on it so much they got sharp again," Xantippus said. "Now don't interrupt me again. F: twenty sesterces for a new wash line—the old one was cut in half; G: a big leg of mutton for a much bigger lion, ten sesterces; and H: two coppers for the use of a piece of my best grade chalk for writing names down on a tablet."

"By Hades, what prices." Julius groaned.

"Quiet!" Xantippus grumbled, apparently unmoved. "All together that makes five hundred and five sesterces and two coppers. You want five hundred sesterces for Udo? Good. Now you still owe me five sesterces and two coppers." Xantippus broke off and looked at his pupils without the hint of a smile.

"We had to spend five sesterces for Udo's new tunic," Publius exclaimed at last. "So we owe you only two coppers."

"Hand it over," Xantippus said.

Tiro had been listening with amusement. "I don't think that is necessary," he said. "My master will assume all outstanding debts with the greatest pleasure."

Xantippus laughed suddenly.

"Then let him just give the boys their money back," he said. "I'm satisfied with the two coppers. As for Udo, I have no intention of keeping him. I'll pay for his release from slavery tomorrow so that he can return to his home in Gaul a free man. That's why I brought him with me; he'd like to give you

all his warmest good-byes. Udo!" he called. "Please come in here now."

Udo entered and bowed before Claudia. He nodded to each of the boys, smiling. "May the gods continue to bless you all," he said.

Caius went up to him and placed both of his hands on his shoulders in a gesture of comradeship. "Thank you for saving my life," he said.

"Ah," Xantippus muttered, smiling in satisfaction. "Caius sees *another* light."

Henry Winterfeld (1901–1990) was born in Germany. He began writing for children in 1933, when he wrote *Trouble at Timpetill* to entertain his son, who was sick with scarlet fever. He went on to write a number of children's books, which have been published around the world.